P9-CSG-261

Shadow on the Mesa

Shadow on the Mesa

Lee Martin

FIVE STAR
A part of Gale, Cengage Learning

Farmington Hills, Mich • San Francisco • New York • Waterville, Maine
Meriden, Conn • Mason, Ohio • Chicago

Five Star™ Publishing, a part of Gale, Cengage Learning.

LIBRARY OF CONGRESS CATALOGING-IN-PUBLICATION DATA

Martin, Lee, 1932–
Shadow on the mesa / Lee Martin–First edition.
pages cm
ISBN 978-1-4328-2962-9 (hardcover) — ISBN 1-4328-2962-9 (hardcover) — ISBN 978-1-4328-2975-9 (ebook) — ISBN 1-4328-2975-0 (ebook)
1. Indian men—Fiction. 2. Mothers and sons—Fiction. 3. Fathers and sons—Fiction. 4. Ranches—Fiction. 5. Murder—Fiction. 6. Revenge—Fiction. 7. Arizona—Fiction. I. Title.
PS3563.A72488S53 2014
813'.54—dc23 2014019534

First Edition. First Printing: October 2014
Find us on Facebook– https://www.facebook.com/FiveStarCengage
Visit our website– http://www.gale.cengage.com/fivestar/
Contact Five Star™ Publishing at FiveStar@cengage.com

Printed in the United States of America
1 2 3 4 5 6 7 18 17 16 15 14

To James Liontas, dean of my law school, whose integrity and honor have been an inspiration, and to my lovely sister Arlene and my brother Don, and further to the memory of our beloved mother, our brother Jack, and our little brother Wesley.

Chapter One

In May of 1883, on the Claymore ranch in the vast prairie of crawling secrets in Arizona Territory, murder was imminent.

The rain gave way to a new and burning sun. The white cliffs were run with crimson, trimmed with dark bristlecone pine and shaded at the base with lofty cottonwoods and whispering aspen. Sage and ocotillo, sharp with scarlet bloom, were scattered in the grassland where occasional cactus seemed lying in wait.

Fresh scents floated in the air at the shallow pond in the wash among the golden blooms of the blue palo verde. In the shade from watchful cottonwoods, a good mile from the ranch house, beautiful Mary Antelope sat down and pulled off her moccasins. In her early forties, she looked much younger. Although Arapaho, she was easily taken as white with skin darkened from the sun. At her side danced a little yellow dog with floppy ears.

"You are so silly," she said, smiling.

A young cowhand with sloppy hat, on guard, sat down on rocks some hundred feet away, both horses on ground-tie. He looked bored and sleepy.

Feeling safe, Mary pushed aside two blankets she had brought with her. Wearing a red gingham dress with her black hair pinned up, her dark eyes were shining.

On a rock across the creek, shaded by a tall cottonwood, a horned toad, flat and spiny, eyes bugging, spat at them and disappeared along the bank.

Mary, embracing every joy in life, was laughing as she stood, lifted her skirts, and waded into the cold water. The little dog splashed around her.

Neither Mary Antelope nor the cowboy on watch were aware of three armed men watching from the base of the cliffs, their presence hidden by trees and brush. Their horses were back against the cliff. One sorrel was snorting, biting at the others. Thor and Clem Welsh were in their forties, with stringy brown hair and dark, brooding eyes. Both brothers wore range clothes and sidearms. Thor had a scraggly beard, but Clem was clean-shaven. They were back shooters for money, and they looked like men who would grind another man's face with their heel for the fun of it.

The third man made them look like weaklings. Rango Welsh, a cousin, was paunchy, dressed in black; he had pale eyes, blond hair streaked with white, and was a throwback to prehistoric times. About forty-five, he wore a thin mustache and trim beard. His skin wrinkled around his eyes and mouth. Rango enjoyed dominance over others. Everything about him was a sign of death.

Rango moved ahead of the brothers, out of earshot, to the edge of the cottonwoods. Thor spat and wiped his mouth with the back of his hand.

"If we wasn't so scared of Rango," Thor said, "we'd hightail it out of here."

"How can he kill a woman?" Clem grunted.

"He hates Wes Montana."

"He's gonna get us hanged."

"Yeah, you and me, we never even met the guy."

"Tell that to Rango."

Thor and Clem were more nervous because they were afraid

of hanging if caught. They were being paid to help Rango track down and murder this woman, but they didn't want any kind of reckoning.

They knew Rango was going to do more than kill her, and his ruthlessness was as frightening as the task. But they were as afraid of Rango as he was of Wes Montana.

They watched Rango start toward the creek on foot. They hesitated. Their cousin was leading them to a noose. They both felt their necks, displaying a horror of hanging. But they were more afraid of Rango and joined him at the creek.

"We'll wait," Rango said. "Maybe that cowhand will ride off."

Down by the wash, Mary Antelope sat with her feet in the water. She picked up the little yellow pup, held it up, then set it on her lap.

"Yes, you are a cute little fellow. My son knew just what I wanted." The pup fussed a bit to get comfortable.

"I'm very happy here," Mary continued. "But I almost died when I was with child. Such a long time ago. Wes and I shouldn't be alive."

The pup squirmed.

"Do you want to hear about it?" Mary laughed. "Yes, you do."

The pup was chewing on her hand.

"It's really the story of Wes Montana."

Mary's story unfolded as the pup grabbed at her dress. It was the beginning of her son's life. Wes Montana, a gunfighter who nearly died before he was born.

Wes Montana was the heart of his mother's story, which for him began in late March 1859.

Mary Antelope was with child and both were at great risk. Wes Montana had little chance of being born alive.

A blizzard raged in the wild Medicine Bow Mountains of southern Wyoming Territory. It was a fierce, driven wall of snow that crushed everything in its sight. Trees fell. Animals and travelers disappeared. Great moving drifts hid tracks and any evidence of life.

In the aftermath, the stillness on a bright morning was shattering. Snow glistened with wet surface from the new sunlight. Ice dangled from branches of weary pine trees.

The crunching of fallen branches startled the silence.

Jedidiah, a thirty-year-old trapper with a heavy brown beard and long dark hair under a fur cap, tramped through the clearing. He wore buckskin clothing under a buffalo robe, and his snowshoes barely skidded on the surface of the snow. His blue eyes were narrowed under heavy brows. His dog, a huge shaggy white mongrel, was leading the way. Behind them, without a lead rope, struggled two mules with heavy packs.

Jedidiah, balancing his long and heavy Sharps rifle, came to a halt as he watched riders approaching through the distant pines.

A dozen cavalry in blue uniforms, huddled under their slickers and drooping, brimmed hats, were fighting their way in the snow. Their pack mules, desperate to stay afloat, followed. Most of the men wore beards to fight the cold.

In the lead, a sergeant with a greatcoat over his uniform came forward and saluted Jedidiah. The sergeant had a short black beard but no mustache. His face was pink from the chill.

"Jedidiah, I thought the blizzard would have done you in."

Jedidiah paused and returned the salute. "Shared a cave with a sleeping grizzly."

"You always were the brave one." The sergeant's brief smile faded as he continued. "Just buried an entire Arapaho village over by Three Rocks. Poor devils."

Jedidiah looked gloomy. "That's where I was headed."

"Maybe you oughta follow along with us, back to the fort."

"I'm headed west."

The sergeant grinned. "Yeah, that's right. You never turn back."

Jedidiah nodded and waved to them as they passed.

Jedidiah had never turned back, ever in his life.

As he watched them head east in the mountain snow, he remembered a young Blackfoot maiden, the only woman he had ever loved. Leaving him to wander the mountains, setting his traps and never inclined, even at rendezvous, to look at another woman. And he had never turned back to Blackfeet country in the far north.

Now he felt like an old man. Even the buffalo robe did not keep his legs from turning to ice sticks.

As he neared Three Rocks, a tall outcropping crusted with snow, he knew he was near the village. Parts of the camp structures were protruding through the heavy snow. It was still and lifeless.

He came upon the common grave. Not how the Arapaho would have wanted it, but they were marked by one big wooden cross. Jedidiah moved around the burial ground. He stood by the cross and said a silent prayer, then crossed his heart.

He moved on, and as the sun rose high in the sky, he was ready to noon in a clearing. He stopped the mules and propped his Sharps on a big rock.

But his dog didn't stop. The shaggy animal crossed over to a snow mound under a lone pine. It began digging, then whined.

Jedidiah picked up his rifle and walked over to stand near it.

"Pepper, what you got? A varmint?" He saw the opening to a hollow interior.

The dog was digging frantically, and Jedidiah set his Sharps aside and bent over to look inside. He saw beads and buckskin.

"My God."

Jedidiah started pulling at the snow to enlarge the opening. A young Indian woman looked frozen. Dead for certain. But Pepper was still whining. Jedidiah reached in and felt her wrist. She was alive.

He straightened, lay his buffalo robe on the snow, and reached in and hauled her out like a log, stiff and barely human. He lay her on the buffalo robe and wrapped it around her. She looked about twenty years old.

He brought the mules forward and made his camp right there. Buffalo chips burned brightly with the usual stench. As she warmed, she opened her eyes.

Jedidiah knelt, a cup of hot coffee in hand. He helped her sit up but kept the robe around her. She managed to sip the coffee.

She was a beautiful young woman. She was more fair than most and had gentle features. Her dark eyes were large and shining.

Jedidiah spoke to her in Arapaho. "All your people are dead."

She seemed to already know and had accepted her loss.

"Your man also," he suggested. She looked at him oddly, as if there was more to tell.

"I'm taking you south to hot country," he told her, still in Arapaho. "To some friends."

She didn't resist or seek to argue. After some broth and bread, she slept by the fire.

Jedidiah watched her with admiration.

In English, he said, "You're a pretty woman, and if I was inclined, I'd offer to marry you right off and take care of you. But I gave my heart away a long time back to a Blackfoot lady. Only she was forced to marry one of her own, and I never looked back."

Jedidiah took good care of her. His shaggy dog watched over her.

★ ★ ★ ★ ★

On the way west, then south, Jedidiah learned her name was Mary Antelope and that she was with child. The father of her child was a white man, she told him in Arapaho. But she could say Ray Eastman in English.

She said Eastman was a trapper who worked with an old man with a red beard and had stumbled on their village the year before. It had been instant love. A marriage ceremony in the village had tied them together.

But Ray Eastman and his partner had gone hunting and never returned. Neither he nor his partner was ever found. He had been unaware she was with child and due in the spring. She refused to believe he had abandoned her.

She grieved for him, but when the latest blizzard tore life from the village, she had taken charge of herself to save her child. She spoke only in Arapaho, except for the name Ray Eastman.

On the way south, Jedidiah did his best for her.

At a trading post, he hitched the mules to a newly purchased but old wagon. They continued south as the first days of spring brought flowers in the meadows. Days were spent teaching her English. She was a fast learner.

Weeks later, Jedidiah brought Mary Antelope down to Arizona Territory. He drove the wagon slowly when he could as she was now very, very pregnant in size.

Mary was in awe of the wide open land. South through Colorado Territory with the Rockies to the east, she often waved her hand at what she saw. Seldom was there a tree, only cactus, sage, and ocotillo. Life was blooming from the scant grass and occasional red earth.

"Sagebrush," she said.

"Right," Jedidiah would confirm.

"Mules," she said, waving at the team.

"Right."

She was a joy to watch as she took in every sight and sound. Birds and squirrels. Red-tailed hawks sailing the sky. Often hot in the day, always freezing at night.

She was becoming more talkative about Ray Eastman and the lovable big Irishman who was his partner.

"Ray," she said, "he was rock."

"Like a rock."

"Yes, and the red beard, he was mountain."

"Like a mountain," he corrected.

Life in the mountains had many more stories to tell.

"We kill the wolves," she said.

"You killed the wolves."

"Yes."

Jedidiah had his own stories, and they became good friends. He shared her grief, not only at the loss of her husband and his partner, but the loss of her entire village and family.

Asleep by the campfire, she had nightmares. He often would reach out and hold her hand, calming her sleep. Jedidiah was also enamored of her, but he had given away his heart, and there was no recovery. He could only remain protective.

At the ranch, Jedidiah and Mary were welcomed by the black-bearded, fifty-year-old cattleman Ross Claymore, who owned a wide open spread that handled some five hundred head of cattle. Claymore had a scar on his left cheek, a crooked nose from injury, and light brown eyes. He was a handsome man in his own right, but his tough life showed in his limited movements.

His pretty wife, Jane, had bright blue eyes, golden hair, and a pink complexion. In her late forties, she was worn but still ready with her smile and kindness.

The Claymores were delighted to have an adopted daughter

and a grandchild. With their only son in the army up north, the Claymores had a lot of love to give. Their kindness wrapped their affection around Mary Antelope.

Jedidiah stayed to await the birth of the child. He and Ross went hunting and fishing and they spent long evenings by the fire.

Jane taught Mary her letters. "You learn fast," Jane told Mary.

Mary helped Jane with cooking and cleaning as much as she could, until she had to stop to deal with the load she was carrying.

And one morning, with Jane's help, she delivered a son.

While Mary Antelope slept by the fire, her child in a cradle next to her, the Claymores and Jedidiah conferred out on the porch where his big dog lay watching everything in sight. The sun was high in the sky.

Jane, seated on the porch swing, was worried. "If Ray Eastman has kinfolk, and they track her down, they could take her son away from her. We must not let her use that name."

Jedidiah, cleaning his rifle, shook his head. "Prettiest place I ever saw was West Montana Territory."

"That's it then," said Ross Claymore. "Wes Montana."

"If she agrees," Jane said.

Jane stood up, gazed around the land, satisfied, and went back inside.

"This gives her a whole new world to fuss over," Ross said.

"I'll be leaving," Jedidiah said. "Back to the Rockies."

"Will you write?"

"I'll do my best."

One warm day after the noon meal, Jedidiah left the Claymore ranch to return to the Rocky Mountains. Watching him from the porch as he disappeared from sight, the Claymores shared the sadness of his leaving.

Mary Antelope, sitting on the porch swing with her child, was even sadder.

"He can't stay long in one place," Ross Claymore said. "He's got a broken heart."

"I know," Jane responded. "But he knows he's welcome here anytime."

"He's a good friend," Mary nodded, her eyes wet.

As time passed, the Claymores doted on Mary and her son, Wes.

Mary was soon welcomed at the church and in the choir. Her joy and goodness were a blessing to all. They judged her as she was, an Arapaho who shared her good heart with everyone. She took care of sick children. She did sewing for the elderly. Everything she did was from the love of others. And Wes was soon in school at the little one-room house painted red.

"Everyone loves Mary," Jane said one night in bed as her husband began to snore. "She does so much for everyone. But I worry about Wes. I know the other boys call him a half-breed."

Jane knew that life was hard for Mary's son. He was neither Arapaho nor white. He was born to a life where prejudice would drive him to fight back. In elementary school, he was taunted whenever grownups were not around. Bigger boys pushed him, bullying, shouting, "Half-breed! Dirty all over."

As Wes grew older and stronger, he would win a fight now and then. But they ganged up on him, often urged on by one of their fathers, an Indian hater with a grudge.

Wes refused to stay out of school, returning home battered and bruised without explanation. His mother let him grow up to be a man, fighting his own battles, but she hurt for him.

One day when he was sixteen, Wes was in the tack room and took down a gun belt. The revolver fit his hand. Ross Claymore walked in and saw he would never get it away from Wes, so he and some of the hands taught the boy how to handle it and use it the right way.

"The first shot," Claymore told him, "has to be self-defense."

Wes practiced day and night until he was so fast, there could be no one faster.

When he wore it to school and showed off his skills at a target pinned on a tree, with even Mr. Grant, the teacher, watching, the harassment stopped. Mr. Grant did not take the weapon from him.

Wearing his sidearm, Wes never again drew it at school. From then on, no one ever again called him a half-breed. By the time he was eighteen, he also learned cattlemen would hire his gun, no questions asked.

He rode off to hunt rustlers in Wyoming Territory. He sent money home, and his mother, who could now read and write, sent him letters. Men he worked with knew he was a half-breed but were not brave enough to mention it. Wes became feared as a hired gun.

Mary ended her story and hugged the little pup as she sat with it on her lap.

"And that's why my son is a great warrior," she said.

She turned to look toward the cowboy on guard. He was asleep in the grass, hat over his face. She smiled.

She drew her feet out of the pond, wrapped a blanket around her, and lay on the grass in the warm sun. The puppy lay with her.

Their lives would end this day in May of 1883.

And Wes Montana's life would never be the same again.

In late June of 1883 in the wistful Big Horn Mountains in Wyoming Territory, it was a bright morning under a clear blue sky. The green hillsides were dotted with purple and gold flowers, even as gunfire echoed in the far eastern canyons.

Ignoring the continued, crackling sound, twenty-four-year-old Wes Montana turned his buckskin south.

He was unaware of his mother's fate in Arizona Territory and longed to be home, to see her smile and hear her laugh. She tied him to the earth and wind. She was the anchor. No matter what happened around him, he always knew she was there, waiting.

It was time to go home. But his gelding continued to toss its head at the distant gunfire.

"Buck, we already quit," Wes said.

Tall, handsome, muscled but lean, and half Arapaho, Wes looked white with a dark complexion. His eyes were dark brown like his shoulder-cropped hair. A thin scar crossed his left cheek. He had a thin, dark mustache and a day's growth of scant beard. He wore dark clothes, a bright red bandanna, a leather vest, and twin holsters with single-action Colts. The left revolver was butt forward.

His wide-brimmed hat was stained and faded from black. It also had two bullet holes in the brim and one in the crown. His bedroll and possibles sack were tied behind the cantle. A lariat was tied with strings near the horn where two canteens dangled as well.

Wes Montana was ready for a long ride. His buckskin balked and tossed its black mane.

"No, Buck, we're going home." Again, the big gelding balked.

"I wrote we was coming."

Wes reached down and stroked the powerful neck. He urged it south.

"You'll get me in trouble."

He had the look of a man to be avoided, hard and unrelenting. A loner, Wes had no facial expression to reveal his thoughts or his next move. His life had been burned into him, leaving no softness, no promise.

Taunted as a half-breed in his early years, he fought back until a six-gun fit his hand so well that he had become the fastest gun in Arizona before he was eighteen. Wes had swallowed memory and hate, but it was still in his gaze, his face, his manner.

His only salvation might be home. He longed to see his mother's smile, to sleep in peace and quiet, to rest from his way of living, to find some other way. She had learned to live with the whites, had become loved by everyone, but it had never happened for Wes. Just the same, he wanted to be with her and the Claymores once again.

He dug in his heels, but the buckskin fought the bit, tossed its head.

"Buck, you ain't listening."

Wes felt more comfortable talking to his horse than to any man he knew. Women, he couldn't talk to at all.

He reined up, hooked his right leg over the horn and drew his harmonica from inside his vest.

"All right. Take a rest."

He glanced up as a golden eagle soared overhead. He tested a tune.

The buckskin tossed its head, ears forward.

More gunfire.

Wes made a face and returned his harmonica to his vest pocket. He put his right boot back in the stirrup and listened intently.

More gunfire, to his left, closer, over the next hill.

The buckskin tossed its head, pawed the grass.

Resigned, Wes took up the reins and turned his horse about, riding the slope until he could see down into a meadow where oak trees lined a creek.

He reined up short.

A smoldering campfire with a discarded running iron. A

heifer, now freed, trotted up the clearing and around a hill, out of sight.

Wes rode down a deer trail.

More gunfire.

When he reached the scene, the fire still smoldered. The running iron had cooled.

The heifer had since run away. Wes reined up to survey the situation. An ugly man with a shield-badge lay dead, flat on his back near his nervous sorrel.

At a nearby tall, barren tree, a teenage boy named Haley, freckle-faced with tousled blond hair, hands bound behind his back, sat in the saddle on his old bay horse. Reins were wrapped around the horn.

Rope dangled from the bare limb above, down to a noose dancing in front of Haley's face. He did not beg, but he looked plenty scared. His blue eyes were round, expectant.

Wes felt an instant knot in his gut. Hanging was an ugly business, and he had seen enough of it. This boy was not going to hang, and Wes was betting his life on it.

Two men were mounted and crowding Haley, both with shield-badges from the Cattlemen's Association. One was the nasty bearded Mason, whose only brother lay on the ground. Mason wore a leather jacket and sweat-stained hat. He believed he was judge and jury. He also hated anyone who was not "pure white," or whole, as he considered himself. Mason hated Indians, Chinese, blacks, or any mixture thereof. He hated anyone with missing or distorted limbs.

And he despised Wes, of whom he was long afraid, until now in his uncontrolled hatred over his brother's death.

The other man was Lomax, an old-timer with a thick, handlebar mustache and a missing left arm from the elbow down. A long-ago cavalry veteran and trail boss on the herds from Texas a way back, he looked weary, reluctant.

Having paid his dues with the cattlemen, tracking rustlers who ended up with a rope, Lomax was fed up, ready to quit. It showed in his weathered face.

Haley's horse stood nervous in the rising wind. Dust blew around them. Mason rode closer to Haley, and reached for the noose.

Haley kicked in his heels. His horse jumped away from the dangling rope. Mason rode closer, grabbed the reins and backed the animal.

Wes rode forward with his six-gun in hand.

"Hold it," Wes said.

Mason spat. "What are you doing here, Montana? You already quit."

Lomax looked relieved. Haley was wild-eyed.

Wes kept his aim on them. "You ran out of hard cases a long time ago."

"They killed my brother," Mason snarled. "And the others got away, but we're hanging this one."

"He's a kid," Wes said.

"We get paid to do a job," Mason argued.

Wes gestured to Lomax. "Free that boy."

"Lomax, you do, and I'll kill you," Mason said.

Wes kept his six-gun on Mason.

With relief, Lomax reached over to Haley and cut his hands free. Haley grabbed the reins.

Mason looked ready to explode. Hating himself for having been afraid of Wes, Mason let his current rage take control. He growled at Wes.

"You got hired for your reputation, Montana, but I figure you ain't so tough." He snickered. "Go on home to your mommy. She still live in a tipi? Maybe I oughta pay her a friendly visit."

Wes looked at Mason and saw a dead man.

Wes gestured to the boy. "Get."

Wes kept his six-gun on Mason.

Haley, eyes brimming, kicked in his heels, set his old horse to a lope, and rode away, along the hillside and over the rise in the direction of the freed heifer.

Wes felt exhilaration when the youth was out of sight.

He slowly holstered his weapon, glaring at Mason. "You was saying?"

Mason smacked his lips. Lomax backed his horse away from Mason.

Realizing he was on his own, Mason tried to feign a withdrawal from the fight. He pushed his hat back with his left hand, but drew with his right.

Wes was faster. He drew and fired before Mason could pull the trigger.

Mason, shot in his chest, his eyes wild, tried to hang on to his weapon, but dropped it. Mason grabbed the horn, tried to stay in the saddle. He buckled, holding his bleeding chest with one hand. He stared at Wes in disbelief, then toppled, dead, from the saddle. As Mason rolled into the grass and lay still, Lomax shook his head and rode forward.

Wes holstered his weapon.

Lomax gestured. "He had one of them new double-action Smith & Wessons. You want it?"

Wes shook his head.

Lomax agreed. "Yeah, they can be tricky. Old Mason shot himself in the boot the other day." He gestured. "Better git afore the others show up."

"Don't want no one dogging my trail."

"There won't be. Everyone hated Mason and his brother."

Wes rode his buckskin forward, reached out to shake Lomax's hand.

"Don't worry, Wes," Lomax said. "I'll make it right."

Wes nodded his thanks and Lomax grinned. "You think that

kid will catch up with that heifer?"

"Sure hope so."

They parted in silent friendship.

Later that day as Wes rode south through the hills, he glanced at his back trail, saw no one but felt it.

He pushed his hat back, all the more anxious to head for home. But he had to know who was following him. He rode out of a canyon, into the trees, and waited.

He had had his fill of killing. He wanted no more. But he sat his buckskin, revolver in hand. Time passed slowly, painfully.

Then Haley, on his old bay horse, came riding out of the canyon. Wes rode out to confront him.

"Mister, don't shoot," Haley said.

Wes slowly holstered his weapon, looking the boy over. "You got a home?"

"No, sir. And I ain't got a job no more."

"Why follow me?"

"I figured you'd get me across the border alive."

Wes could see the boy had no sidearm, but there was an old rifle in his scabbard. The bay horse was really old.

"How old are you?" Wes asked.

"Fourteen."

"You know anything about cattle, besides a running iron?"

"Yes, sir, before my pa was killed."

"Maybe you can get work. In Arizona Territory."

The boy brightened.

Wes wasn't used to company, but he figured Claymores would welcome the boy.

On the way south, Wes learned more about the boy.

At their camp one night, a coyote howling in the distant

grasslands, Haley, whose first name was Jim, talked about his family.

"My mother died when I was born," he said, "back in Ohio."

Wes listened as he stirred beans in a hot pan.

"My pa was a schoolteacher, but he couldn't teach anymore, so we came west, tried to start our own herd with mavericks. He said the law said it was okay."

Wes served beans to Haley as he held up his tin plate.

"But it got so we come on a branded calf, we'd use a running iron." At Wes's frown, he nodded. "I know, big mistake. So the cattlemen, they hunted us down about two years ago. They shot my pa, but they let me go."

Wes filled his own plate.

"I wore one of those badges," Wes said.

"But you were never one of them."

"No, and I quit."

Haley downed his beans as if he had never eaten.

"My pa was a good man," Haley said. "And when he was gone, I fell in with some other fellas looking for mavericks. But when we got shot at, they left me behind. That's when they was gonna hang me."

"What are you looking for now?"

"A job," Haley said. "I still want my own place someday."

"What about school?"

"My pa taught me until he was shot."

After a time, the boy looked more comfortable.

"What about your folks?" Haley asked.

"Never knew my pa. But my mother's waiting." Wes shrugged. "She's always waiting."

"Maybe I'd have turned out better if I'd have had my mother."

"Didn't keep me out of fights."

"Yeah, you ain't afraid of nobody."

"It's a long time growing up," Wes said. "And I don't figure we ever get there."

"Not even old men?"

Wes shook his head. "Not even old men."

Wes and Haley arrived in Arizona Territory late that September. Aspen on the forested mountains were already gold.

They headed for the Claymore ranch as they crossed semi-desert country. Mixed cattle with a few white faces were roaming the hills. Bunch grass. Scattered cactus. A prairie dog rising, darting out of sight. And a big turkey buzzard circling.

It was hot, but a breeze was rising.

Crossing the prairie with its silver sage and unfriendly choya, they saw the sudden rush of gold and tan as a dozen pronghorn antelope sprang into view and scattered like bouncing rabbits until they were out of sight.

Haley, still riding his old brown horse, was beaming. With no family, he had latched onto Wes, but what he really longed for was the home he had lost when his father had died.

Haley remembered milking the cow and getting kicked or swatted by the tail, riding herd with legs too short for the stirrups, building corrals, hunting and fishing with his dad. He knew he had a long wait until he could marry and have his own family.

"I sure do like Arizona," Haley said, more than once.

Late in the day, Wes and Haley could see the white and crimson cliffs, shaded in spots by pine, quaking aspen turned gold, and cottonwoods.

They rode at a dog-trot pace as they approached the weathered, single-story Claymore ranch house. Lazy oaks with dark shiny leaves cast shade around the buildings. There were no signs of ranch hands but cattle grazed the far hills. Two old horses were in the corral, standing in the shade of the barn.

Wes felt a rush of memory. He had lived here as a boy, a wild boy fighting everyone and everything until a six-gun fit his hand. Yet there had been more, riding, roping, branding, and trail drives. Riding broncs to a standstill had gained the respect of the hands.

As Wes and Haley approached the ranch house, Ross Claymore, now seventy-four, came outside. Claymore, gray-bearded, weary, lame, wearing worn but clean britches and a faded blue shirt, looked anxious and sober. A lifetime of work showed in his weathered face and dark eyes. His gray hair was scant.

Mrs. Jane Claymore, petite in a blue dress and heavy shawl, gray and bent, using a cane, appeared in the doorway behind him.

A pretty woman just shy of her husband's age, she looked weary, but at the sight of Wes, her face lit up like the sunrise.

"It's Wes," she said, then looked tearful.

Ross was grim. "I sure hate having to tell him."

She nodded, but she trusted her husband to do his best.

They stood waiting as Wes and Haley rode up.

Wes, happy to be home, dismounted, and shook the old man's hand. He hurried over to hug Mrs. Claymore.

Wes was happy. "You both look the same."

"You lost your badge?" Claymore asked.

"I quit."

"Glad to hear it."

Wes turned, nodded to Haley, who was still mounted. "This is Jim Haley. He's got no folks. Needs a job."

The Claymores brightened. Haley tipped his hat.

"Jim," Claymore said, "you get over to the bunkhouse. The cook shed's in back of it. Swanson's the foreman. When he comes in tonight, he'll put you to work. All right?"

"Yes, sir, thank you, sir."

Haley was happy and had wet eyes as he turned and rode his old bay horse over to the corrals.

"Nice boy," Claymore said. "But he's got the oldest horse I ever did see."

Wes looked around. "Where's Ma?"

Claymore took a deep breath. "Behind the house. With our son."

Wes caught his breath, realized what Claymore was saying. He looked stunned, devastated.

"Did you get my letter?" Claymore asked.

Wes shook his head, mouth tight.

"She was murdered," Claymore said.

Mrs. Claymore started to cry and went back inside.

Claymore fought for his words. "A cowboy we sent to watch her down at the wash got his throat cut. It was dirty business, Wes. And ain't a day gone by we ain't been sick over it."

It was too much for Wes. His heart was pounding. Sweat broke out on his face. He put his hand on a porch post, steadied himself. He turned his back to Claymore; he could hardly breathe. The world was on his shoulders. His legs were about to give way. He fixed his gaze on the old horses in the corral.

His mother's beautiful face flashed before him. Weeks and months had not dimmed his memory. But he had been gone far too long.

Claymore spoke quietly. "About three months ago. My foreman found her dead at the creek. She was treated pretty bad. There were tracks of three men, but the posse lost their trail."

Wes was so angry, he could not speak.

Remembering his own pain whenever his mother so much as had a splinter in her finger, Wes could only fight the burning inside of him. The thought of her being hurt by the three men, what they must have done to her, was a knife twisting in his heart. Wes had never shed a tear in his life, but now he was close. He let go of the post, clenched his fists, and pulled his hat down tight. His hands fell to his holsters for comfort.

Claymore choked on his words, swallowed hard.

"Even killed her little dog." He fought for his voice. "Sheriff put out handbills, but no luck. Don't figure they was local. Weren't nothing to go on, no how." Claymore shook his head. "Don't know the reason, but in white women's clothes, she didn't look much Arapaho, just sun darkened, so I don't figure it was that."

Wes's face was darker by the minute. He tried to swallow the rage building up within him.

As twilight fell, Claymore led the way around the house to the two graves with board crosses. Their son had died at Fort Donelson. His marker read TOM CLAYMORE, 1830–1862.

On Wes's mother's grave, it read MARY ANTELOPE, 1838–1883.

Wes, hat in hand, crunched it. His eyes burned with guilt, remorse. He should have been here.

Late that night, it was dark behind the house except for lamplight through the back window. The air was cold, bitter.

Wes sat on a stump near his mother's grave. Alone with a broken heart, hat in hand. In his vivid memory, he again saw her face: a beautiful Arapaho woman, with long, lustrous black hair tied up around her head to look less Indian. Smiling, loving.

He shook himself free of the memory. He reached in his pocket, took out his harmonica, and began to play the traditional ballad "Red River Valley." Softly. Talking to her with his music. Her favorite tune.

He stopped, rubbed his eyes, pulled his hat down tight. Too choked up to continue, he slid the harmonica into his pocket. He sat long into the night, gazing at the stars, letting the cold penetrate his clothes, bring bumps to his skin. He wiped his eyes with the back of his hand.

In the morning, Wes, fully clothed with boots off, awakened from the cot near the cold hearth. His hat had been covering his eyes. He sat up, rubbed his eyes, and looked around.

The house was simple in design. There was a stack of wood by the hearth. Oil paper covered bad spots on a wall. The wooden floor and mostly handmade furniture were dusty, worn.

Wes smelled the coffee on the iron stove. He pulled on his boots with effort, as his feet were still swollen from the heat. He set his hat on his head.

Claymore's rifle, along with some oil and a ramrod, rested on the table. Claymore, fully dressed, sat down to finish cleaning the rifle. The smell of gun oil on the rags was pungent. He nodded to Wes, showing his sympathy and his own sadness.

"Jane's still asleep," Claymore said. "She took it pretty hard."

Wes stood up. He strapped on his twin holsters by habit and tied them down. He took a cup of coffee from the battered pot off the iron stove. There was a hot pan of bacon and beans next to it.

Ignoring the food, he forced himself to sit down at the table. He sipped the hot coffee, then stared into his cup.

"I thought I'd come home," Wes said. "Take better care of her, change my way of living."

"Didn't matter to her, Wes. She figured you was a warrior, and she trusted you to do right."

Wes fell silent.

After a time, Claymore finished cleaning his rifle. "Wes, you recall as to how your ma was brought here by Jedidiah, an old friend of mine?"

Wes nodded.

"And how he'd found her in a snow cave in the Medicine Bows?"

Wes sipped the hot coffee, not paying much heed.

Claymore cleared his throat. "There's a little more to it."

Wes fondled his cup, stared into the steam.

"First off, we said your pa's name was Montana."

Wes looked up, watched Claymore, and listened.

"We made it up. She thought he was dead and was afraid your pa's kin would come and take you away, being his only son."

Wes listened, and waited.

"But now's she's gone, I figure you ought to have the whole story."

Now he had Wes's attention.

"She told us as how your pa was Ray Eastman. They were married in an Arapaho ceremony over in the Medicine Bows in Wyoming Territory."

Wes was interested, but it didn't change anything. So his history was different. She was still buried in the back yard. She was gone, and no story would bring her back.

"What you don't know is," Claymore said, "your pa, he had a partner, an older man, a big Irishman named Bob Riley. The two of them took off on a hunting trip. She didn't want to hold him back, so she never told him she was with child."

Wes leaned back, watching Claymore, and listened.

"The two men never came back, so she figured they was dead. And it wasn't long afore the blizzard of fifty-nine wiped out the whole Arapaho village. The army come along and buried 'em."

Wes looked drained. He leaned forward, staring into his cup.

Claymore cleared his throat. He got up, refilled his coffee cup, and came back to the table. He sipped his coffee, searching for the rest of his story.

Wes was trying to concentrate on what Claymore was saying, but in his grief, new information was hard to swallow. He stood up and walked to the window, his back to Claymore. It was all the more painful as Claymore continued.

"Not long after, Jedidiah left his traps and was heading down the mountain when he found her in a snow cave. He brung her all the way down here. We took good care of her, the best we could."

Wes continued to stare out the window.

"My wife taught you both to read and write." Claymore leaned back. "Your mother sang in the choir. No one thought of her as Indian on account of she was an angel to everyone, helping out with the children and newborns." He cleared his throat. "Folks for a hundred miles around came to her funeral."

Claymore hesitated, then continued.

"But you had a different life. Kids called you names. You beat up some of 'em. But then you grew up and got to be fast and a good shot, so they left you alone. You rode off and hired out your six-gun. You even got yourself a reputation. Nobody dared call you a breed after that."

Wes wasn't hearing anything new at the moment, so he was losing interest, even as Claymore continued.

"Now, Jedidiah, when he brought your ma here, he was on the run himself. He had a broken heart over some Blackfoot woman up in Montana Territory. So he wandered about, moved his trap lines all over the Rockies, year after year."

Claymore paused, sipped his coffee, then continued.

"Jedidiah was trapping in the southwest Colorado Rockies, not far above the mesa, when he discovered that your pa, Ray Eastman, had a ranch above Falls Creek." He hesitated. "Seems maybe he up and abandoned your ma on account of he went south and never looked back, spent time in the army, and married up with a widow woman. They have a son."

He had Wes's attention now. Wes straightened, bit his lip. He rested his right hand on his holster.

"Jedidiah, he wrote us about it and where Eastman was. So I helped her write a letter to your father. Just said she was still alive and living here, and how she had his son. Even gave your name as Wes Montana."

Wes, raging inside, waited for Claymore to continue.

"Never got no answer," Claymore said.

"When was it mailed?" Wes turned, his face tight, eyes narrowed.

"A few weeks before she died." Claymore shrugged.

"So he knew she was still alive. And who I was."

Claymore shrugged. "Could be he never got the letter."

"If he did . . ."

"He's got a wife and son. And a big spread. Maybe he wanted to make sure no one ever found out he'd married an Arapaho. Course it weren't legal under white man's law, but it could have made a lot of trouble for him."

Wes was on fire. He sat down as if the wind was knocked out of him.

Claymore hesitated, studied Wes, then got up and walked over to a metal box on the shelf. He brought it back to the table and sat down.

"Wes, your ma made me promise . . . something in here she wants you to give your pa." Claymore opened the box.

He took out her small medicine amulet, about the size of a pocket watch. It was bound in soft deer hide and dangled from rawhide string.

Wes winced at the sight of it.

Claymore handed the amulet to Wes, who recoiled from its touch, but let it rest in front of him on the table as Claymore continued.

"He made this for her. Carved that pronghorn on it. She said if you showed it to Eastman, he'd know it came from her. It'd prove you were his son."

Wes's face showed his growing fury.

Claymore leaned back. "She told me that was the symbol of safety, life, existence."

"Didn't save her, did it?"

"Thing is, she wasn't wearing it. She gave it to me to keep for you, right after she wrote the letter."

Wes clamped his hand around the amulet.

"If he did this, I'll kill him."

"Don't make no wild guesses," Claymore said.

"I'll make sure." Wes opened his grip to stare at the amulet. "Then I'll kill him."

"Jedidiah's the only friend you'll have over there, so I'd find him right off. He may have some more information by now."

"What about the Irishman?"

"Bob Riley? He was pretty old at the time. Probably died a long time ago."

Wes looked away, the amulet in his hand.

"Wes, one thing to remember. Eastman's son may know nothing of you, but he's still your half brother."

Wes knew that, but his mind was on his father, a man he might have to kill.

Mrs. Claymore came out of the bedroom. Wes got up to help her to her chair.

Chapter Two

Weeks later, Wes rode north toward Falls Creek, southwestern Colorado's high mesa country. It was late in the day. His buckskin moved faster without a hot sun bearing down on them. Grass was taller. Trees in fall colors, mixed with dark pine, were everywhere. The sun was low in the west.

Every sound was increasingly loud. The creak of his saddle, the chomping of the bit, every hoofbeat on the hard soil. The smell of his horse's sweat mingled with his own.

The small cattle town rested on a flat at the lower edge of the southern, high mesa country, facing the Rockies to the east. Snow caps rose beyond the rugged hills and dark timberline. From the far-off mesa, a tall waterfall jumped its way down the rocks and to the wide pond and creeks below. Nearby, smaller falls trickled down. A stream wandered near the town. In all other directions, there was the lone prairie.

Wes knew he was getting closer to the day he might have to kill his father, a man he had never met. His Colts had never felt heavier.

The town had one street with a few stores, one saloon, a livery, and no sign of the law or a church. The buildings showed signs of wear from snow and wind. A dozen horses lined the rails, mostly in front of the saloon. A wagon stood empty in front of one of the stores.

Wes Montana reined to a halt in front of the swayback general store. A sign stated that the store also served as the post office and stage depot. A hand written sign read POSTAGE NOW 2 CENTS. Another read NEXT STAGE TO SALT LAKE: MONDAY.

Keeping his right sidearm clear of his long coat, Wes dismounted and draped a rein over the railing. His buckskin nuzzled him. Wes drew his old rifle from the scabbard.

"We're here, Buck," he said softly. He surveyed the empty street. An old black dog was trotting toward the saloon. It crawled under the boardwalk in the shade.

Wes entered the cluttered, well-stocked store. Barrels were everywhere. Shelves with cans. Boots hanging from the ceiling. Clothes on racks. Big Stetsons on the wall for ten dollars. Handmade boots for twenty. Six-guns under the glass-faced counter. Rifles on the wall behind it. Bull Durham. A corkboard had stage times and notices.

Elmer Bates, a man in his sixties, was the proprietor. He wore crooked spectacles on a round nose, was neat with clothes well-pressed, had not much hair, and was a bit skinny. Pleasant, easygoing, friendly. He sat on a chair near the stove, reading a newspaper. He looked fascinated by everything he read.

Even as Wes walked around the store, Bates kept reading and now read aloud for Wes's benefit.

"John L. Sullivan. What a fist that man has." Bates paused, looked up at Wes. "I'm Elmer Bates. What can I do for you, son?"

"Looking for Ray Eastman."

"You planning to work for him?"

"No."

Bates folded the newspaper. "Good thing. Gonna be a range war up there on the mesa. And some Rodecker men are over at the saloon now. Watch out for them. It's Saturday night, you know."

"Rodecker?"

Bates stood. "Eastman moved in on the south end of the mesa when the Utes was forced out, about two years ago. He figured the whole mesa was his. But the Rodeckers moved in on the north side with too many head, crowding him. There's a river separating them, and there's creeks, but Eastman's water on the south side is what Rodecker's really after. And all that tall grass."

Wes studied the clothes on the rack.

Bates continued. "Three of Eastman's hands were run off some time back. And two more were found shot a couple weeks ago. No proof who done it, but things are gonna explode right soon."

"No law around here?"

"Not in a hundred miles, and our letters don't get answered. They either don't give a hoot, or they got their hands full. Reckon we're too far south on this side of the Rockies and too small to get any attention. Howsomever, the railroad done got across to Grand Junction up north. Maybe times will be a-changing."

Wes looked at a new Stetson. Some handmade boots.

"Eastman, he got some army contracts to sell his beef. Funny enough, one's for the Utes, now they're on reservations, and more with Fort Lewis. Rodecker's got some, but he wants 'em all."

Bates studied Wes a bit more. He could see the hardness, the tied-down holsters, the unrelenting gaze. He cleared his throat and continued.

"You want to get to Eastman's, head east along the creek. At the falls, you'll see the wagon road to the right. Only easy way up on the south side. Eastman blasted it open."

Bates paused to gesture. "You get up on the mesa, the river runs center of it, all the way from the falls to the mountains. Just turn right."

Bates grunted, continued. "Eastman, he got himself a snooty wife. She pays my wife to make dresses for her, on account of store bought ain't good enough. And they got a useless son. But Eastman's either rich, or cattle poor, depending how you see it."

Wes tried on the hat, liked it. He seemed uninterested in Bates's description of the Eastmans, but inside, he was burning with every bit of information.

Bates folded the newspaper. "But the best thing he's got up there is Rosalie Ann Riley. Her grandfather was Eastman's old partner. She's an orphan and had no one, so Eastman took her in maybe four years back. She's Irish and a real handful. But I tell you for sure, she's real gosh-awful beautiful."

Wes worked the lever on a new Winchester. He liked it. Put his old rifle on the counter as a trade.

Bates chuckled. "All the young fellas for a hundred miles around are hankering for her, but it ain't only Eastman keeps them away. She's a darn good shot herself."

Wes, wearing the new hat, walked over to the counter with the Winchester, set it down. He handed over his old hat with bullet holes in the brim and crown, startling Bates. Bates moved behind the counter, took the hat, and put it out of sight as if to discard.

Wes studied the shelves behind Bates. "I'll take the hat and rifle. Two boxes of shells. Some coffee. Peaches."

Wes paused to look over the glass bottles holding striped candy. He took three, stuck them inside his vest pocket.

Bates started piling up the purchases.

Wes spotted a long heavy coat. He tried it on, liked it.

"You'll need it up there," Bates said.

Wes added it to his purchases.

Then Wes noted the folded paper. "Only newspaper you got?"

"Just the one. Goes over to the barber next. And you know

what? President Arthur's pushing the navy to make ships out of steel. Can you believe that? And the army done followed Geronimo down into Mexico. Times is just moving too fast."

Wes put gold coin on the counter. "You know a trapper named Jedidiah?"

Bates nodded. "Sure, he lives in the high mountains. The Razorbacks, we call 'em." He paused to complete the order. "Don't see him much. But for sure, in the spring when he brings down his furs. Don't pay much these days, but it's a way of life. Don't figure he'll change."

"Know how to find him?"

"He told me once, he doesn't want to be found. Never takes the same trail twice. But he did let it slip that he lives near a needle rock that gives him the time of day, like a sundial."

Bates followed Wes outside to Wes's horse. Wes slid the new Winchester into his empty scabbard. He slid the coffee and peaches in his possibles sack, put the shells in his saddlebags, and tied the new coat onto his bedroll. The buckskin nuzzled Wes.

Wes turned to Bates. "You got a hotel in this town?"

"Nope, just the livery down the street. But you can eat at the Big Dollar Saloon."

Wes stepped up and into the saddle.

Bates gazed up at him, curious. "You look like a fella who's carrying the whole world on his back and then some." Bates hesitated. "Mind telling me your name, son?"

"Wes Montana."

Bates stared in dismay as Wes turned his horse down the street. Bates, shaken, watched him until he reached the livery.

Of a sudden, Bates went back inside, retrieved Wes's shot-up hat from the throwaway box. He put his finger through the bullet holes, reshaped it, hung it on the wall behind the counter.

He took up the old rifle Wes had traded and stood it in the corner.

Bates was in awe. "Wes Montana," he murmured.

Wes left his horse at the Falls Creek Livery with a young, freckled boy of ten, who happily took his dollar and a piece of striped candy. Then Wes washed up at the trough and headed for the Big Dollar Saloon.

As night fell, Wes sat eating at a table at the Big Dollar Saloon with his back to the side wall. The saloon was busy with heavy drinking, smoke, and noise. There were eight card players at two other tables.

An old piano player with wiry mustache and a cigar in his teeth hit bad chords. There were no women. Not even paintings of them. However, high on the wall behind Wes was a huge painting of a longhorn bull, side view but head facing toward the room. Wes ate in silence, his stomach churning over the task ahead.

Make sure. Then kill his own father. Nothing else would ease his pain. He paused to look around the saloon.

Nearby were two drunks, heads down on their table. They smelled of whiskey and sweat. There were men at the bar, but now the saloon was mostly empty and quiet.

Quiet was hard on Wes. It allowed too much memory, too much pain. He cleaned his plate and sipped his coffee. He appeared not to notice the three men at the bar. Everyone in the saloon was a stranger to him, but he could sense trouble. Trouble he had no time for and found of no interest.

One of the men was Kid "Lightning" Holloman, midtwenties, pink-faced, swaggering. He wore a fancy red vest and an old hat. He looked like trouble. Drinking too much. Laughing. A braggart backed by arrogance. A showoff who liked to intimidate. His sidearm was well-oiled in a cut-down holster.

Kid suddenly turned, drew fast, fired a shot at the painting over Wes's head. It hit the bull between the eyes.

Wes showed no reaction. He sipped his coffee. He seemed unaware, didn't look up.

The piano stopped. The noise stopped. Men turned to stare.

Kid Lightning laughed. "Bull's-eye."

The two drunks didn't move, heads still down. Four men at one table got up and left the saloon. The other four card players kept at their game but were plenty nervous.

The mustached barkeep paused, annoyed. "Lightning, you're gonna pay for that."

Two men crowded around Kid Lightning, laughed with him.

One of them was the bearded Josh Miller, an ugly man in his thirties who looked like he hadn't bathed or washed his clothes in a year. He had stringy hair, crooked eyebrows, and a nasty laugh. He didn't really like Kid Lightning, but he had trouble making friends with anyone else.

Another, Potluck, in his fifties, sported a poorly trimmed mustache, had red cropped hair and crazy gray eyes, and looked like a comic. He made a lot of faces to make others laugh. He wore an oversized shirt and baggy pants. He didn't mind being in Kid Lightning's shadow. It made him feel bigger and smarter.

All three were intoxicated.

Miller gestured at the painting. "You think that's something? I'll chop off its tail."

The barkeep started to protest further, then thought better of it. He backed away, busied himself at the far end of the bar.

Miller was too drunk to draw fast. His gun wavered in his hand. He fired, three times with clumsy fanning of the hammer. His shots missed the painting. The bullets slammed into the wall two feet over Wes's head.

Kid Lightning laughed, fired, and shot a hole in the bull's rump.

Wes still did not look up. There was a hush.

Kid Lightning was annoyed. "Hey, mister, ain't you scared?"

Miller waved his hand. "Yeah, this here's the Lightning Kid. He'll part your hair if he's got a mind."

Wes continued to sip his coffee, and did not look up. The three rowdies were laughing and drinking.

Bates entered and walked to the bar, stood some distance from Kid Lightning and his friends. Bates stared at the goings-on and backed away. He joined the barkeep at the far end of the bar.

"Hey, Bates," Potluck said with a chuckle. "You're just in time for the show. The Kid's gonna part that fella's hair."

Bates ordered a drink and backed around the end of the bar, ready to duck behind it if necessary. Bates didn't like his town being a battleground. Didn't like rowdies scaring customers away. He was a businessman. He and the barkeep exchanged nervous glances.

The three rowdies at the bar studied the silent Wes, who seemed unaware of them.

Potluck grinned. "I bet I can get his hat."

Kid Lightning made a face as he reloaded his revolver. "You'll skin his head. Better let me do it."

Kid Lightning checked the chamber, holstered his six-gun. He moved away from the bar. He made a big show of it as he threatened Wes. His eyes were dark and crazy to create fear. Wes wasn't taking the bait. Men scrambled to get out of the line of fire.

Wes slowly got to his feet.

Kid Lightning postured. "Aw, you moved."

Wes slid his coat away from his right sidearm. His dark, narrowed eyes had the look of a man who could easily kill and then walk away without looking back. A man to reckon with.

The rowdies were not quite sober enough to recognize the threat.

Miller laughed. "Hey, Lightning, he wants to play."

The barkeep raised his voice. "Not in here, you don't."

"All I want is his hat," mused Kid Lightning. "Dead or alive."

Kid Lightning started to draw.

Wes's six-gun leaped into his hand. He took aim at Kid Lightning's forehead. His gaze was cold, deadly.

Kid Lightning stopped in amazement, weapon only halfway clear, realized he was about to die. He slowly let his six-gun slide back into the holster. Kid Lightning was appalled.

Wes held his weapon steady, aimed at Kid Lightning.

Miller caught his breath. "Holy cow. He beat you, Kid. I mean, did you see that? You was almost dead. And still owing me five dollars."

Kid Lightning swallowed hard. "Only 'cause I ain't sober."

Wes kept his weapon level. There was high tension and a fearful hush.

No one dared move.

Until Bates pulled himself together. He looked right at Kid Lightning.

"Hold on. Don't you know who that is?" Bates paused for effect. "That's Wes Montana." The onlookers were stunned.

Potluck, Miller, and Kid Lightning, struck with sudden fear, were frozen. Kid realized he was lucky to be alive and wiped his mouth with the back of his hand.

Wes, six-gun in hand, moved along the wall to the swinging doors, his weapon aimed at Kid Lightning.

Wes watched them as he moved outside.

They kept staring after him. At the swinging doors.

Miller whispered. "Lightning, you wet your britches."

"Shut up," Lightning muttered.

Potluck made a face. "Geez, who would have figured."

Lightning adjusted his gun belt. "Next time, we'll be ready for him."

"Yeah, he's only one man," Potluck said, sweating.

"But he ain't the kind you take face on," Miller said.

At the end of the bar, Bates hid a satisfied smile.

Wes was relieved he did not have to shoot anyone in Falls Creek. It was the first time in a long while he was glad his name could make others back away.

He spent the night in the livery with his buckskin. It was not easy to sleep, wondering what his father looked like, what kind of a man he was.

Pigeons rustled on the rafters, made soft cooing sounds. Mice ran through the loft, scattering hay.

Wes would have preferred silence, but hearing life moving about was not so bad, either. But each time he closed his eyes, he saw his mother's face, heard her laughter, felt her gentle touch. His anger at her loss of life was never going to heal, not until the killer was dead.

Wes did not rise early. He was in no hurry to confront the man who was his father, a man who might have murdered Wes's mother.

Wes had a good breakfast at the empty saloon, then saddled up and left in the late afternoon. He could not bring himself to hurry to the business of maybe having to kill his own father.

But his mother's brutal murder would torment him forever, eased only by the death of those responsible. It was grinding inside of him like loco weed.

Wes knew about death. It had haunted him from the first day he learned he could handle a six-gun better than anyone else. It followed him everywhere and struck fear in all who heard his name. For good reason.

Now he was on his way to another fight. It was a long ride to and across the dry mesa. As Wes rode, he formulated anger at

Eastman, whether or not the man was guilty, because Wes had been cheated out of having a father. Growing up, it could have made a difference.

The Claymores had been good to him and his mother, but there had been no real closeness, and he knew it was his own fault.

A boy needed a father. Maybe if Mary had wed another, it might have been helpful, but she had left her heart in the Medicine Bows. There had been only one love in her life, and she had refused to believe, as Wes did, that Ray Eastman had abandoned her.

Even if Eastman hadn't known she was with child, why didn't he return?

His new life on the mesa told Wes that Eastman had never intended to go back to his marriage with Mary Antelope. That belief was also eating at Wes.

The late afternoon sun cast Wes's shadow forward as he rode east on the south side of the shallow river. Soon he turned his buckskin south, wary of what was to come.

On the height of the Mesa and south of the river that ran east to west, the Eastman ranch at early morn was a beautiful sight. Rugged country but with plenty of dry feed and distant ponds. Scattered pines, golden aspen, cottonwoods along the river. Cattle, horses grazing. Three mule deer, one a magnificent buck, darted into the far trees. A golden eagle sailed across the blue sky.

Beyond the mesa, the Razorbacks rose straight up. The mountains were black at the bottom where they were covered by forest, crested with glistening snow at the top, rocky and steep. The wide but shallow and rocky river meandered west from the first cliffs, splitting the mesa.

Wes knew he was on Eastman land. It chilled him.

Time would tell if his father was guilty. It might take longer for Wes to drive himself to kill the man. He wondered if he could do it, and then he thought of his mother's violent death. There was no question. Ray Eastman would have to die.

Wes reined up. He was in no hurry to face it. He could see his mother walking through that tall grass, turning to wave and smile, her long black hair glistening in the sun, someone who hadn't deserved a terrible fate.

And his father was going to pay the price.

Before Wes's arrival, it was quiet on the south half of the mesa. Eastman's faded, two-story frame ranch house, with veranda and a wide porch, and not-so-pretty flowers along a picket fence, was set away from the corrals and buildings.

Cattle and horses grazed in the distance where two riders circled them. Three colts frolicked in the corral by the barn. Smoke curled from the bunkhouse chimney. There was the smell of biscuits, burned bacon, hot coffee.

Inside the Eastman ranch house, the parlor had a large stone hearth with dwindling fire. A plush sofa was out of place in the tired room. Old furniture and a worn rug were more fitting.

In her room, Rosalie Riley, all Irish, twenty and gorgeous with long, flowing red hair and dark blue eyes, wore a dark blue riding outfit with full skirts. A tan wide-brimmed hat dangled on her back from a chin strap. With soft, pink skin and a few freckles, a slight tilt to her pretty nose, a fearless gaze, and a woman' figure, she looked like every man's dream.

Rosalie paused to fondle the glistening rosewood music box on her dresser, all she had left from her mother. Her parents, dead of fever, had given her a happy life. Their death had left a vacancy in her heart. She lifted the box lid, let the music play softly.

It was suddenly painful and she closed the lid quickly.

She picked up the tintype of her parents, the faded portrait still bringing tears to her eyes. Her mother had loved her in every way. Her father had protected them both. She had been happy, but at sixteen, she had found herself alone. Alone and fighting to overcome it.

Rosalie wanted love, a husband and children, a family to replace the one she had lost. Ray Eastman was kind to her, and he could be a father substitute except his wife was a pain and always making trouble.

She reluctantly left her room. She walked through the parlor and headed toward the door. She was in a hurry.

Too late.

Mona Eastman—in her late forties, a bit chubby, snooty, well-dressed, and handsome, with blonde hair in tight waves—walked into the parlor. Mona's heritage went all the way back to fine English traditions. But there was something dark behind Mona's chilled blue eyes, as if another woman lived inside. She did not like Rosalie, did not like her living in her house. Perhaps there was a bit of jealousy for Rosalie's fresh beauty.

Mona saw her own life as a disappointment and fully resented Rosalie's daily joy.

Rosalie tried to get to the front door. Mona caught up to her.

"Where do you think you're going?"

"Riding with Chuck."

"You're a bad influence on my son."

"We're just riding, Mona. He's like my kid brother."

Mona backed off. "Two men were shot in the hills. It's not safe."

"You go to town by yourself."

"It's the other direction, to see my dressmaker." Mona looked put upon. "And I have trouble getting away for that, with Ray crippled up."

"He'll be up and around before you know it."

"Just remember your date to picnic with Art Rodecker."

"I'm not happy about it."

"You're so ungrateful. I never asked to take you in. That was Ray's idea. But this is my house, and you will listen to me, or I'll send you away."

Rosalie was immediately defensive.

Mona caught herself, tried harder to sound reasonable. "Do you see any other eligible young men within a hundred miles? No one wants Irish, but if you marry Art, you will be accepted."

Rosalie, angered, took another step toward the door.

"Mona, I'm proud to be Irish."

Mona moved closer, caught her hand.

"This is hard country, and men control everything. That's why I try so hard to help you." Mona drew herself up. "May I remind you again, a lady would have her hair nicely set? You look like a wild Indian."

Rosalie started to leave. Mona held onto her hand.

"Art Rodecker is a fine young man. He's educated, handsome, and he has a rich father."

"Who's squatting on the mesa."

"If you marry Art, there'd be no fighting."

"I have no interest in him, not that way."

"Give it a chance." Mona paused to lay on more guilt. "Or maybe you are too selfish to remember how much I've done for you. You were a sixteen-year-old mess when you came here. And for four years, you've been living in this house. I did not have to accept you. We could have refused help, sent you away when you had no place else to go."

"You kept sending me away to school."

"To make a lady out of you." Mona sniffed. "Is it so much to ask that you give Art a chance?"

"I will give him a chance." Rosalie stood waiting for that hug she had never been given.

Instead, Mona freed her hand and backed away. Rosalie took a deep breath.

They heard loud men's voices down the hallway. Mona made a face. "That's Chuck, fighting with his father."

Rosalie moved to the door. "I'll wait for him at the corral." She slipped away and out the door.

As the door closed behind Rosalie, Mona glared after her. Alone in the parlor, Mona walked to the ornate wall mirror and fussed with her hair. She turned sideways to admire her figure. She smiled at her image.

Chuck Eastman, seventeen with unruly brown hair, hurried into the parlor from the back hallway with hat in hand. Handsome, husky, clean-shaven, and a bit awkward, Chuck wore a sidearm but did not appear to be aware of it. It was just hanging there at his hip. His ranch clothes hung a bit loose.

Chuck wanted nothing more out of life than to earn his father's approval, but it seemed less likely than ever. Looking upset and angry, he stumbled to a halt in front of his mother. He adjusted his hat.

"Charles, have you been fighting again?"

"All I ask is to be treated like a son."

"But he is your father and you have a nice easy life here. What's wrong with that?"

Chuck yanked at his hat. "He doesn't trust me with anything on this ranch. He treats me like a kid."

"He won't always be around, you know."

Chuck managed a grin, shook his head. "He's going to live forever. Horses fall on him. He gets shot. He goes off a cliff. And he's still here."

"Trust me, Charles, and keep your head."

"Why doesn't he like me?"

"It's not you. He's getting old and resents your youth and strength."

Chuck digested her words.

"Ma, do you know what really gets to me?"

"His being so uncivilized?"

"How much I want to be just like him."

Mona glared at him. "Don't be foolish."

"I mean it, Ma."

"Your father came from nowhere. He was a foundling. He was nothing before the War where he was made an officer."

"But he worked hard after that, and he got this ranch. Be proud of him, Ma."

"You forget. My family dates back hundreds of years in England. They were among the aristocracy."

Chuck grinned. "But we're all Americans."

"You just don't listen."

Chuck shrugged, then charged outside.

Mona glared after him.

She loved her son because she had given birth to him, but sometimes she resented him. He made her older than she wanted to be. Her beauty was fading. Every time she looked at him, she felt older. She returned to the mirror. Turning her head, she admired herself. She deserved a better life than she had.

At the corrals on the Eastman ranch, Chuck saddled their horses as Rosalie played with the old yellow dog by the watering trough.

His was a bay gelding. Hers was a sorrel mare with a sidesaddle. He tightened the cinches. Over in a far corral, two men were working two horses. Otherwise, it was a quiet and peaceful day.

But Chuck was still smarting from the fight with his father.

Maybe Chuck was too easygoing, too carefree, too happy-go-lucky, and maybe he should take the ranch more seriously. But why? There were plenty of hands even after Rodecker scared some away. Chuck didn't matter on the place.

Chuck had never been given any responsibility. He was less necessary than a fence post, a cocky kid who would do anything for his father's respect but felt he would never get it. Worse, his mother didn't seem to care about him except as a target for her discontent.

So here he was, riding again with his best friend, Rosalie. Oh, she was older and a girl, but she knew him well enough and accepted his flaws.

Rosalie left the yellow dog and came over to Chuck. She stopped, turned, and looked back toward the house. She looked hurt.

"Your mother doesn't like me."

"Nah, she just hates living here. She takes it out on all of us, even Ray. She wants him to sell out, but he won't do it."

Rosalie was still frowning. "If I had this ranch, I'd be dancing on the clouds."

"She wants to go to Denver, live high off the hog."

"What about you?"

Chuck grinned. "Well, I could find me a wife in Denver."

"You're a kid."

"I'm seventeen, geez."

They both laughed.

Chuck still grinned. "Nah, I like it here. And I got you to pick on. It's like having a big sister, even if you are a peck of trouble and always sassing me."

"You're an easy target."

He helped her up on the sidesaddle.

"This is a monstrous way to ride," she said.

"But you're a girl." They both laughed as he mounted.

As Chuck rode on ahead, she reined up to look back at the house.

She recalled the moment she had stood on the front porch with her luggage. The moment Mona laid eyes on her. Mona's phony smile, the continued harassment from then on while fawning over her in front of Ray.

She turned her horse and set it into a trot, then a lope, aiming to catch up with Chuck, her very best friend.

Chapter Three

In the late afternoon, Wes rode onto the Eastman spread. His heart was heavy with what he had to do.

A father who had abandoned him before he was born and who had arranged for Mary Antelope to die to protect his ranch, his image, his family, to avoid shame. Shame at having looked at an Arapaho woman. Bitter, Wes moistened his lips. The more he thought of it, the more it was turning him into a killer.

He gazed around. The ranch buildings and corrals were well-kept. The house was fading, but had some flowers and a picket fence. Yes, Eastman had a fine spread and was well-to-do. No wonder he did anything he could to shut out the past.

As Wes rode closer to the barn and corrals, a yellow dog barked at the end of its rope near the tack room. Men at the corrals turned to watch. There was hammering from the smithy.

Wes felt his insides churn, his face burning. The dog kept barking a moment longer, then stopped, watching Wes as if they were old friends and wagging its tail.

As Wes approached the smithy, housed partly in a shack, an old man came outside. His clothes were scrubby, worn, his old hat pushed back from his forehead. He scratched his beard with a hoof pick. He was seventy, with a casual but deliberate air about him. He wasn't big or husky, but it was obvious no one talked back to him.

Wes reined up in front of him.

"You lost, mister?"

"Looking for Ray Eastman."

"I'm Sam Jones. I do the hiring."

"This is personal."

"Who are you?"

"Wes Montana."

Jones spat into the dirt. "So it's come to that. They got hired guns. Now we got one."

Wes did not respond.

"Well, Mr. Eastman got busted up a couple weeks ago when a horse fell on 'im. He's inside the house."

From the corrals, Shorty McCall, older than Jones, shuffled over to have a look at Wes. Shorty had a hairy face with a poorly cropped mustache. He wore old range clothes as if he was one step from the saddle. He had clear blue eyes that twinkled. He was also lame.

"What's going on, Sam?"

"Wes Montana here. Wants to see Ray."

Shorty grinned. "That'll liven things up." He looked Wes over. "Kind of young, ain't you?"

"Shorty, you talk too much," Jones said.

"Maybe so, but he can sure even the odds. Young Sanders was in town last night. Seems Wes here buffaloed three of Rodecker's men."

"Which ones?" Jones asked.

Shorty grinned. "Lightning, Miller, and Potluck. Lightning drew on him, but Wes here was faster."

Jones grinned. "I gotta hear about that."

They both looked at Wes, who shrugged.

"They sure won't forget it," Jones said, sobering, "but Wes, they won't be giving you a chance from now on."

Wes liked these two old men but wasn't happy being the subject of conversation. He had stayed alive keeping to himself.

Jones sensed Wes was embarrassed and liked him for it.

"Well, come on, Montana," Jones said, "but I don't figure Mrs. Eastman will let the likes of you step one foot inside."

Jones led the way over to the house. Shorty shuffled along behind him and Wes. Shorty was plenty amused and Wes wasn't sure why. Maybe he liked things stirred up.

Wes reined up at the railing in front of the picket fence. He dismounted and draped the reins over the railing. With pounding heart, he walked with Jones and Shorty through the little gate and along the walk. They went up the steps to the front porch and Jones knocked on the front door.

The door opened at length.

Mona Eastman, cold and unfriendly, stood in front of them. She knew she was attractive but didn't care to impress these men. She hated to be bothered by the likes of them, they were so far beneath her.

Annoyed, she was in no mood for company. It showed in her face, and lesser men would have retreated. She was the boss's wife, but she wasn't the boss.

She glared at Sam Jones, then at Wes and his dark narrowed eyes. He almost frightened her. Almost.

"Yes?"

Sam Jones leaned forward. "Mrs. Eastman, this here's Wes Montana. He'd like to see Mr. Eastman."

Mona recognized the name, swallowed her surprise, and remained cold. She hid well the rage rising within her, the nerve of this man showing up.

She glared at Wes. "Mr. Jones does the hiring."

"I'm not looking for work," Wes said.

Mona acted as if she was going to shut the door in his face.

"I have a message for Mr. Eastman." Wes removed his hat. He did not flinch under her glare.

Mona was biting her words. "From you?"

"No, ma'am. From the Claymore ranch, Arizona Territory."

Mona swallowed the further surprise, looking him over with disdain.

"Mr. Eastman was badly injured. He's resting."

"Ma'am, I'm not leaving until I see him."

Mona glanced at Sam Jones. At the curious Shorty. With no way out, she turned to Wes.

"Well, come in then."

Mona let Wes inside and closed the door on Sam Jones and Shorty. She led the way into the parlor then turned to glare at Wes.

"Mr. Eastman was hurt by a horse. He can't get up. Just give me the message."

"Sorry, ma'am. I have to deliver it in person."

Further irritated, she moved toward the hallway.

"Wait here."

Wes turned toward the sofa. She spun around.

"That's a Louis XV sofa. Please do not sit on it. You're too dirty. Just stand over there."

Wes stood, hat in hand. She turned into the hallway and then the first room on the left. Within earshot.

Wes felt on fire. That man in that room. His father. A stranger. A man who had abandoned him and his mother before he was born. A man who may have had Wes's mother murdered to cover his tracks.

But worse than that, Wes had had an empty spot in his life. Although the Claymores had given him a loving home, he had felt more like a visitor with one foot out the door. His own fault perhaps.

But Wes had grown up without his own father to take him fishing, tell him about life. Target shoot with him. Hunt. Talk long into the night. Wrestle with him, laugh with him. Never there to tell Wes that being half Arapaho was something to be proud of, a challenge to the world.

Now that man was in the next room. A man he might have to kill. Wes tried to be calm but his heart was out of control. He could hear the conversation.

Mona spoke clearly. "Some young man is here. He's from the Claymore ranch. Arizona Territory."

A man's gruff voice, his father's voice, was loud.

"I bought a good horse with their brand. I'll talk to him."

Wes moved closer to the hallway. He listened intently.

She sounded sweet. "You shouldn't see anyone in your condition."

"I ain't lost my hearing."

"You can hardly move. You're hurt inside."

"Send him in. This is man's business."

"The doctor said you should rest."

"You're not making it any easier."

"As your wife, I forbid you to alarm yourself."

Eastman's voice rose. "Ain't you listening to me? Send him in here."

"You needn't shout."

There was a shuffle of Mona's dress and footsteps. Wes moved back and away from the hallway.

Mona came into the parlor. She glared at Wes.

"At your own risk."

Mona stood aside, looking snooty.

Wes could not move for a long moment. Hat in one hand, other near his right holster, he could barely get his breath.

This was the man who left his mother to die in a blizzard. Who may have sent killers to silence her. Wes forced one foot in front of the other.

Mona led him to the room where Ray Eastman, a gruff man in his fifties, sat on a chair by the window, his left leg resting on a second chair. A crutch leaned on the wall next to him. He was cleaning a Winchester repeater.

With unkempt dark hair, square jaw, and flashing blue eyes, Eastman looked mean and ornery. Clean-shaven with thick brown hair to the collar, he wore ranch clothes and boots, as if determined not to be crippled. Everything about him looked combative, a grizzly of a man.

The room was nicely furnished, but there was a saddle on a rack. Ropes were stacked in a corner on the deep carpet, and a gun belt hung on the bedpost near him.

Wes held back his anger. He entered the room alone, the door open behind him.

He fought for his words.

"Mr. Eastman?"

Eastman studied him. "And you are?"

"Wes Montana."

Ray Eastman considered the name, made a face.

"I heard of you. The cattlemen hired you for some trouble up north. What's that got to do with the Claymore ranch?"

Eastman settled back, watched Wes.

"Mr. Claymore asked me to tell you . . ."

Wes drew a deep breath and came right out with it. "Mary Antelope is dead."

A long throbbing silence. Eastman's face quivered; his eyes narrowed. He looked explosive as he tried to sit up straight.

Wes waited, his heart racing.

Outside, in the hallway, Mona, who was standing close to the door to listen, put her hands over her mouth.

In the bedroom, Eastman looked ready to reach for the pistol in his gun belt, hanging near him. Wes, filled with anger and vengeance, could not read the man.

Eastman was grim. "Mary Antelope died more than twenty years ago."

"He said she wrote you a letter, a few months back."

"What?"

"A few weeks later, she was murdered."

"I told you, she died. In a blizzard, a long time ago."

Wes hesitated a long moment. He shook his head.

"She's buried on the Claymore ranch."

"That's a lie." Eastman tried to stand. His injuries hindered him. He looked angry as Wes made ready to leave.

"What kind of a game is he playing?"

Wes did not know what to believe. His right hand rested on his holster.

"Mr. Claymore figured when you got her letter, you sent men to track her down and kill her."

"Where is this Claymore?"

Wes was forced to lie to protect Claymore. "He's dead."

"And a dead man sent you?"

"His last request."

Wes turned to the door, hurrying to get away.

Ray Eastman was furious. "I ain't finished talking to you!" Eastman roared. He tried to get up, but nearly fell and sat back down. "Montana, you get back here!"

Wes made it out the door, down the hallway, past the frozen Mona, and made it to the front door. He exited before she could react.

Mona hurried in to calm Ray Eastman.

"Ray, you're going to hurt yourself."

"Get him back."

"There's no need."

"He said my Mary was alive a few months ago and sent me a letter. Was there a letter from a Mary Antelope?"

"You're being foolish, Ray."

"Was there?"

"Of course not. Besides, could a dirty Indian write a letter?"

She backed away from Eastman's fury.

"How'd you know she was Indian?"

"With a name like that?"

"She was Arapaho, but—"

"Ray!" She tried to be calm. "I'm your wife now. We were married by a preacher. And I gave you a son."

"Yeah, well, what kind of game is Montana playing?"

"He was lying. That's how they do it. Get you to believe them, and then ask for money."

Eastman realized she could be right. He shrugged, settled down.

"Maybe so."

"You know it's true."

"Yeah, you're right."

Eastman leaned back, shook his head. "And I know better," he said.

But even knowing he had indeed lost his Mary so many years ago, Ray Eastman was full of yearning for the past, a time long before he was in the War, primitive days in the high country when all that was between a man and survival was his rifle. And all that was between him and the cold of night was a woman.

Mona left him alone to brood.

Ray was in a lot of pain from his injury, but there was something even more painful in his heart. He sat staring at the sunlight streaming through the window.

He had many regrets in his life, none more painful than any thought or memory of Mary Antelope. He had learned to compromise in life, but that young hired gun had torn open his wounds. He wanted to kill him for the hurt that now raged within him.

Outside, Wes reached his horse, took up the reins and led it away from the picket fence. His face was running with sweat. Traumatized, Wes was about to fall apart. The sun was low in the west. He felt the chill on his hot body.

Jones stood in his way. Shorty was next to him. They had heard the yelling when Wes was inside. Both old men loved Eastman, and they liked Wes. They felt a kinship to Wes, despite his way of life. Maybe it was because they could tell he liked them in return.

Jones grinned. "You deliver your message?"

"In part."

Shorty gestured. "You can't get anywhere tonight, young fella. May as well bunk with us."

Wes shrugged. "Don't seem like a good idea."

Jones couldn't stop grinning. "We'll hide your horse. You can sleep in the shed behind the smithy and leave at sunup."

Shorty nodded. "Still some grub in the cookhouse."

There was only silence from the house.

Wes looked from one to the other. He was still smarting from the trauma of meeting his father, of not getting an answer.

But Wes liked the two gruff old men. He liked being around them, feeling their age and knowledge and experience, like a warm sun. Abruptly, the sound of hoofbeats broke the stillness.

Wes, Shorty, and Jones turned to watch two riders approaching from the hills to the north. The sun was sinking in the west, casting long shadows. In the lead was Chuck Eastman, acting goofy in the saddle. He waved his hat and raced ahead of Rosalie.

Rosalie looked gorgeous, with rosy cheeks, hat dangling down her back from the chin strap, long red hair blowing in the wind. Even sidesaddle, she looked a part of her mount.

The riders nearly crashed into the corral fence, sending the three men scattering, as the horses slid to a halt.

Away from them, watching the two laughing riders, Jones, Shorty, and Wes were silent a moment.

Jones spoke. "That's Chuck Eastman."

Wes swallowed hard. This youth was his half brother. A nice-looking kid, happy, the way Wes had never been. Had Eastman taken Chuck fishing and hunting? Had he talked long into the night with the boy and shared his wisdom and history? Had Eastman known how to love a son?

Jones broke into his thoughts. "Rosalie, there, she was an orphan, maybe sixteen, when she come here a few years back," Jones told him. "Her grandfather was Bob Riley, an old friend of Mr. Eastman, but Riley died in the War. When her folks died of fever, everything was burned."

Wes stared at Chuck and Rosalie.

Jones continued. "Mr. Eastman insisted on taking care of Rosalie so his wife could make a lady out of her."

Shorty grinned. "Didn't work."

"That girl ever gets hitched," Jones said, "her kids would be something to behold. And run from."

They watched Rosalie and Chuck poking fun at each other.

Jones shook his head. "Mrs. Eastman got fed up, sent her to finishing school. She got kicked out a few months ago and came home, and not the first time." Jones grinned. "A lot of devil in that girl."

Chuck and Rosalie stepped down and turned their horses over to the men at the corral.

Chuck poked at Rosalie. "One of these days I'm going to leave you out there."

Chuck and Rosalie, their laughter subsiding, turned to gaze at Wes. And Wes looked long at Chuck, his half brother. Rosalie was still poking Chuck and teasing him, but Wes was getting her attention more and more.

The sun was low in the west. It set her hair on fire. Chuck and Rosalie stopped laughing. They walked over to Jones, Shorty, and Wes. They stared at Wes's cold, hard face and narrowed eyes. Wes, at least a foot taller than Rosalie, towered over her.

Rosalie saw more in Wes than his pent-up rage. The lines of his handsome face, the way he stood like a statue, his gun belt ready, the air about him dark with danger. A knight without his shining armor. It pleased Rosalie to think so.

Wes could see she was far too beautiful—a young woman a man could fight over, pursue, with no chance of subduing her spirit. A right attractive challenge. But he was not for her.

Jones gestured. "Chuck, Miss Rosalie, this here's Wes Montana."

"The gunfighter?" Chuck asked, startled.

"The big bad man," Rosalie said with delight.

Jones kept sober. "Don't worry. Mr. Montana's gonna ride out first light. Right after chuck."

"Pity," Rosalie said with an interested smile. Chuck poked her, then looked at the solemn Wes.

Rosalie looked Wes over and smiled. Jones showed his disapproval.

"Don't look so mean, Mr. Jones," she teased. "I can handle you." She turned and smiled flirtatiously at the silent, grim Wes. "And you, Mr. Montana, you don't scare me."

She laughed, walking away with Chuck. Chuck and Rosalie poked at each other and hustled toward the house. Wes, Shorty, and Jones watched until the two were on the porch.

Jones grunted, turned to Wes "She's right about me."

Shorty grinned. "Yeah, she can turn us both inside out."

Wes felt a knot in his middle just from meeting her, but he was half Arapaho and not in her world. Besides, he had other things on his mind.

On the porch of the Eastman ranch house, in the twilight, Chuck and Rosalie turned to look back as the three men headed for the smithy with Wes's buckskin.

Rosalie wrinkled her nose. "That's the coldest man I've ever met. Did you see those really, really dark eyes? I don't think he even breathes."

"They say he kills men just by scaring 'em to death."

"Maybe it's true."

Chuck postured with humor. "Yeah, he's a mean one, all right, but I could take him."

"Don't be silly. You'd get blood all over you."

Rosalie walked to the front door, paused, and looked back to where Jones admired Wes's horse.

She smiled. "Still, it might be fun to wake him up. He might even be handsome, if he didn't look so mean. I like him." She giggled. "Maybe I'll marry him."

"Ma's got other plans for you, remember?"

"If Ray knew she wanted me to marry a Rodecker, he'd have a cow."

"If she knew you was all squishy over a hired gun, she'd send you back east again, or lock you up."

Rosalie made a face. "She's not my mother."

"But she sure is mine. Oh, boy, is she." They laughed and walked in the house.

At the smithy with Shorty and Jones, Wes looked toward the Eastman house. He could barely handle his question.

"This Ray Eastman, what kind of a man is he?"

"Ornery. Real ornery. And hates being laid up." Jones scratched his beard. "Colt he was breaking, it rolled right over him. Crippled him up pretty bad this time. He has to keep proving himself."

"Yeah," Shorty said. "I think he does it to make his wife mad."

Wes, eyes dark and narrowed, watched the house.

Jones shook his head. "I've set one of his legs or arms every four or five years." He grinned. "She's been trying to make a gentleman out of him for a long time. It ain't gonna work."

"More to him than that," Shorty added. "He gives you his word, that's it. I've never known him to turn his back on anyone asking for help. Honest as they come."

"Just don't cross him," Jones said.

Shorty grinned. "Yeah, he's pretty trick on the trigger."

Wes decided this was just everyday admiration from men who liked their boss.

"And his son?" Wes asked.

Jones stretched, yawned. "Chuck, he ain't good for much, but we like him. He makes us laugh. And he can take a ribbing."

"And Bob Riley?" Wes asked.

Jones took a moment. "All I know is, he was Rosalie's grandpa. Used to trap with Mr. Eastman when they were young. They rode a lot of trails together. Partners. Both wore blue in the War between the States, but right off, Old Bob took a cannon ball, died from it."

Wes, leading his buckskin, walked with them, around behind the shack that housed the smithy. There was a small corral.

Wes was hearing good things about Ray Eastman. It didn't seem to fit what he believed about him. It wasn't anything he wanted to hear.

"So where you headed?" Shorty asked.

"Looking for a trapper called Jedidiah." Wes paused, wondered. "Mr. Eastman ever trap with him?"

"No," Jones said. "I don't figure they've ever met. But I've seen Jedidiah in town. He's kind of a hermit."

Shorty nodded. "A throwback to the old mountain men."

"He's up in the Razorbacks," Jones said. "But nobody knows where. And there ain't no trails."

"You'll get lost up there," Shorty said.

"He's right," Jones said. "Better off you stick around and go fishing with us. There are some good, fat trout about now. And we could get in some elk hunting."

"Maybe later," Wes said.

Wes liked these old men more than he had planned. Men who had earned their mark in this wild frontier. He found himself wondering if they had been in the War between the States. If they had prospected, rode with the trail herds from Texas, been married and fathered children, if they had loved ones far away.

But his reason for being here overshadowed everyone and everything. He turned to unsaddle his buckskin.

"We'll get you some grain," Shorty said.

He watched them walk away.

"Well, Buck," he said softly, "we're here, and I ain't sure of nothing."

Later that night after chuck, Wes, unable to sleep, walked to the front opening of the shed. He stood staring at the lights in the ranch house. His agony was on his face. He came to kill a man he found himself liking. He adjusted his hat, smoothed his hair, and grimaced.

Slowly, he turned and walked back. No lamps were lit in the shed. The moon was bright, casting a glow inside. Near the open doors, Wes sat on an upright barrel, holding the amulet, staring at it. Finally, he put it away in his vest pocket and took out his harmonica. It was his only source of peace.

He wondered if Ray Eastman remembered that Mary Antelope's favorite tune was "Red River Valley," from the days Ray would sing to her in the village, probably the only story his mother had ever told him about his father. At least that he could remember. Maybe he would get the hint, charging outside to ask more questions. Or maybe Mona Eastman was sitting on him. Just the same, Wes needed to express himself.

As he played "Red River Valley," he watched the house. His

music was soft but easily heard beyond the shed.

Wes was startled as Jones walked in with his guitar. Jones did not say anything. He sat down and joined in with "Red River Valley" on the guitar. Shortly after, crotchety Shorty walked in with a fiddle, sat down without a word, and sawed away.

The three men never spoke. Each would choose a tune, and the others would pick up on it. They played many songs, the music drifting into the night. Some of the ranch hands came out of the dark bunkhouse and sat on the bench in front, listening.

On the dark veranda on the second story of the ranch house, Rosalie, in her robe, stood listening. Chuck joined her in his stocking feet. They enjoyed the sound drifting in the night.

Chuck shook his head. "I can't believe a man like that can play music."

"He makes my heart sing," she said.

Chuck, startled by her words, shrugged.

Rosalie spoke softly. "I think Wes Montana is going to change everything around here."

"Not if Ma has anything to say about it."

"Your mother wears me out, Chuck."

"Yeah, me, too."

Rosalie gestured. "They sound like they've played together for years."

They smiled, leaned on the rail, and listened.

Chuck made a face. "Montana doesn't talk much."

"He's talking to us now."

In the Eastmans' bedroom by lamplight, his boots off, Ray leaned from the bed, listening through the open window. The music was drifting toward the house. Pleasing music.

Mona, still dressed, came in fussing and walked over to close the window.

"Leave it open," he said. "It's a good sound."

"You'll catch a chill."

His voice rose. "I said leave it open."

"You don't have to raise your voice."

"Leave it be. I haven't heard those boys play for a long time." He listened a moment. "Who's on the mouth organ?"

"I really don't know. And it's called a harmonica."

"You find out about Montana?"

"I told you, he's gone," she lied. "That's all I know."

She glared at him and walked out of the room.

Eastman grimaced but enjoyed the music as he lay back.

Late in the evening, as the music stopped, Rosalie and Chuck went back inside to retire.

At the smithy shed, Shorty and Jones packed up their instruments, nodded to Wes, and headed back to the bunkhouse without a word.

Chapter Four

At daybreak, Wes left the ranch, riding north on the dry mesa and over to the wide but shallow river. He wore the heavy leather jacket from Bates's store; his bedroll and possibles were on the back of his saddle, over which his slicker was tied down.

Wes stayed on the south side of the river, turning right and riding east across the mesa toward the Razorbacks. He had ridden some distance from the ranch when he found he had company. Wes reined up by instinct, and turned in the saddle.

Riding after him at a lope was Rosalie. She wore riding clothes and a wide-brimmed, man's hat with chin strap. She rode sidesaddle on a bay mare. As usual, she was something to behold.

"Buck, we're in a lot of trouble." He waited and could not help but enjoy the sight of her.

She reined up short, her horse sliding to a halt near him. His buckskin jumped and snorted. She smiled brightly.

"Sam Jones said you were riding to the Razorbacks."

"Alone."

"I'm going with you."

"No, you're not."

Wes started riding toward the mountains. She came up alongside him, still smiling.

"You can't stop me."

He set his heels to his mount, into a lope. She laughed and did the same.

Finally, to save his horse, he slowed it to a walk. She was at his side like a bad penny. He was torn between irritation and pleasure. No man could stay angry long at Rosalie.

She chattered on as they rode.

"They won't let me go up there. And no one will take me. So I'm going with you."

He kept riding, trying to ignore her.

She bubbled on. "They say you can see for fifty miles. Even the red hills of Utah."

Wes was quiet awhile, then turned to her. "Your grandfather was Bob Riley?"

"Yes, he died before I was born."

"He had trapped with Mr. Eastman?"

She hesitated. "Yes, before the War."

"In the Medicine Bows?"

"Yes, up in Wyoming Territory. My father said my grandfather saved Ray's life in a blizzard. But that's all I know."

"He ever mention Ray Eastman having been married at the time?"

"I don't remember anything like that. Why are you asking?"

"No reason."

"Wes Montana, you're a man who has a reason for everything he does. Now what is it?"

Wes fell silent as she glared at him.

"I'm going to have to teach you some manners."

He ignored her remark, but there was no ignoring how she looked in the saddle, hair blowing about her pretty face.

The wind was rising to greet the sun. Grass rustled and dipped. Trees seemed to sway. It was a beautiful day for a ride. They both fell silent to enjoy it.

But not for long. Dark clouds were rising over the far mountains, casting new shadows, bringing a sharp chill. As they neared the rise of the Razorbacks, there was no clear trail; every way up was steep and looked impossible.

Back at the ranch, Chuck, unable to get his father's approval, visited with his mother. He was having coffee with her in the parlor. Maybe, just once, she would say something nice about him. Except he was never on her mind.

She had a throw over the fancy chair on which he sat. She made a face at his dusty boots and clothes. She was sitting prim and proper on the fancy sofa.

She held her cup like a lady. "Where's Rosalie?"

"I heard her go out, afore sunup."

"I told her it wasn't safe."

"The hands look out for her."

"That girl needs to be locked up." Mona shook her head. "There's too much of Bob Riley in her. Too much Irish."

"What's wrong with the Irish, Ma?"

"Back in New York, there were signs all over, saying, 'We don't hire Irish.' There had to be a reason. And my family looked down on them."

"I don't figure it."

"Just take my word for it."

"But Rosalie's a sweetheart."

"No, she's not. And finishing school was a waste."

Chuck grinned. "Yeah, she said they were too prissy."

Mona saw no humor in it. Shook her head. "She doesn't appreciate what I try to do for her."

"You can't change people, Ma."

"Not that girl anyway, but she has to be nicer to Art Rodecker."

"Ma, she—"

"It's to keep the peace. Give her a position in society. And avoid a range war."

"She won't do it, Ma."

"She'll do as she's told."

Chuck couldn't help himself. He had to say it.

"Not after she got a look at Wes Montana. She's set her cap for 'im."

Mona stood, turned her back, and pretended to fix her hair in the mirror. She drew herself up, worked her lips. She seemed to be swallowing information she didn't want to face.

"Sit down, Ma. I was only funning. Besides, Montana took off for the Razorbacks. Won't never see him again."

"He must never come back here."

"He won't," Chuck said, watching her with some confusion.

"We must keep him away from his father."

"His father?"

Quickly, "I mean your father." She sat down, sipped her coffee. "He upset Ray. I think he was trying to get money out of him."

Chuck grinned. "Lots of luck there."

"You don't know how hard it's been, trying to civilize your father. Ropes and saddles in the bedroom. At least he doesn't wear his spurs to bed." Shook her head. "I asked for a Steinway piano so Rosalie could practice. He won't listen."

"She's the one said no."

"What? That girl."

"You can't change either one of 'em, Ma."

"She's twenty years old. A spinster."

"What about me? Am I an old bachelor?" Chuck was grinning. She was not amused.

"You are just a boy. Enjoy it while you can."

"I can do a man's work."

"Stop." Mona tensed, looked stricken. "I can't deal with all this."

"Don't take life so serious, Ma."

"I have no choice. That terrible man, Montana, he's got your father talking about a range war."

"Ma, it's already here. Somebody's scared off some of our men. We found two of 'em dead. We been losing cattle. Montana never started that."

"But he is dangerous."

Chuck puffed up. "I'll straighten him out, he ever comes back."

"You stay away from him. They say he's killed a dozen men. That kind has no heart. He even looks like a half-breed."

"Where do you get that, Ma? He looks white."

She backed off, quickly. "Maybe I'm wrong."

She got up and walked out of the room without another word.

Chuck was left empty, with an aching heart. He felt no one on the ranch, save Rosalie, even cared if he was alive.

Later that morning, Ray Eastman, fully dressed and wearing his sidearm—a way of fooling himself that he'd soon be well—hobbled onto the porch with a cane and sat down. He pushed his hat back and waited for Jones, as he had sent for him.

It was sunny, but dark clouds hovered over the distant Razorbacks to the east. Jones walked over and stood on the steps.

Jones and Eastman had an unspoken friendship. They could count on each other. There was mutual respect.

"I heard music last night," Eastman said.

"Yeah, my old guitar and Shorty's fiddle." Grinned. "And Wes was playing the harmonica real sweet."

"I thought he rode off last night."

"Early this morning," Jones said. "He was gonna look for that hermit Jedidiah, but he won't find 'im."

"That was real sweet music."

"Yeah, he really likes 'Red River Valley.' Played that several times."

"I heard." Eastman made a face. "I'm not so sure he isn't looking for money, from some things he said."

"I don't know nothing about that, but Sanders was saying as how he was in town Saturday night and saw Wes back down Rodecker's men. Lightning and Miller and Potluck were drinking too much. Lightning drew on Wes but was beat hands down, didn't even clear his holster. When Bates said he was Wes Montana, Lightning wet himself." He grinned. "Right in front of everybody."

"I'd sure like to have seen that," Eastman said.

"Except they won't be giving Wes a chance next time."

"I want to talk to him."

"I don't know if he'll be back," Jones said. "Think we should hire him?"

"You trust him?"

Jones grinned. "Yeah, and all we'd have to do is say his name. The whole West is afraid of him."

"Are you?"

"No, I ain't. When he plays his harmonica, you can see he's really a good kid. He looks mean all the time, but we like him."

"All right, if he comes back, hire him." Eastman looked around. "Where's Rosalie?"

"She went riding early this morning." Hesitated. "She may have caught up with Montana. But don't worry, she's got too much sense to get in trouble."

"You'd better hope so."

That same morning, Wes and Rosalie made it to the foot of the Razorbacks. A series of waterfalls led down to the river into creeks and to the ponds to the south.

Rosalie was happy. Being with Wes, mean as he tried to be, was a lot more pleasurable than being with Art Rodecker. Wes represented another life, another world far from the mesa. She liked him and was intrigued.

Wes wasn't used to being with a woman at all, but if a man had to have one for company, he couldn't find a more enjoyable or more gorgeous one than Rosalie. She made the sun a lot brighter. As they rode, she chattered and pointed to birds and rocks. Wes tried to ignore her, but it was impossible.

The darkening sky was a warning, but they kept riding. From time to time, they rode through some of the cattle, leaving their tracks mingled, but without intention.

They left the last creek but stopped at the foot of a steep, impossible climb. Wes studied the terrain, looking around.

Rosalie gestured. "There's not even a deer trail."

"This here's as far as you go."

"I'm going with you. And you can't stop me." She turned in the saddle, looked north. "But they might stop you."

Wes followed her gaze. Five men rode toward them.

She sobered. "That's Art Rodecker in the lead. He wants to marry me. The two right behind him are the Welsh brothers. Hired killers. And Chuck says they're mean when they drink too much. They have a really bad cousin, he said. Rango."

Wes didn't know the Welsh brothers, but he knew Rango. Up north in Virginia City, Wes had nearly got Rango hanged a year back, but the man had escaped. Wes knew that Rango swore vengeance, but it was equally well-known he was afraid of Wes and had found some other territory in which to make trouble.

Wes sat quiet in the saddle, watching them approach.

Art Rodecker was in his thirties, good-looking, clean-shaven, arrogant, well-dressed and outfitted. He had slick hair, a small trimmed mustache, and the air of a dandy. His hat was small-brimmed. His eyes were pale blue and intense. Art rode a chunky bay gelding.

He shared his father's ambition and greed, but he didn't let it show when he was around Rosalie.

Thor, bearded, and Clem Welsh, mean-eyed, looked as if they had never seen Mary Antelope. They had a gift for killing and forgetting. And they would take money for anything.

The other two men, Lehman and Motry, both in their fifties, looked like hardened gunmen who had never turned a steer. They had day-old beards, evil dark eyes under heavy brows, and soiled hats. Both had their holsters tied down. They were all business.

The five, Art in the lead, reined up in front of them. Art tipped his hat, and smiled at Rosalie, only. "Miss Rosalie, good morning."

Rosalie smiled. "Art Rodecker, Wes Montana."

Art was not surprised, having heard about what had happened at the saloon. He appeared unimpressed.

The Welsh brothers hid their sudden dread. They leaned on the pommel, both slightly intoxicated. They knew how dangerous Wes could be, and they had enough guilt to fill a barn, but they felt safety in numbers. Lehman and Motry held back to the rear. They were likely the most deadly. Men you couldn't turn your back on, not for a second.

Art showed his displeasure. "Mr. Montana has quite a reputation."

"All talk," Lehman said, riding forward.

Art smiled again at Rosalie. "Maybe I'd better escort you back to the ranch."

"Oh, dear, no. Mr. Montana is taking me riding."

Art looked up the steep grade, at the Razorbacks.

"Not up there, he's not."

"Just up to the rise, so I can see the view."

"There's no way up there."

"I'm not worried," she said.

Art frowned. "I assume Mr. Eastman knows where you are?"

"Of course."

Motry rode up a little closer to look Wes over.

"He don't look so tough," Motry said. "Lightning must have really been drunk." He smirked at Wes. "His eyes, they're hollow."

Wes sat quiet in the saddle, his dark eyes gleaming.

Lehman nodded. "Yeah, he looks easy to me."

Motry spat. "Look at 'im. He can't talk."

"He was talking up a storm," Rosalie said, "before you came."

Art took up his reins. "Maybe I'll go with you."

Rosalie's chin went up. "Aren't you a little far south, Mr. Rodecker?"

Art Rodecker hesitated. He took her remark seriously. He turned, looked to the dark clouds hovering over the Razorbacks.

"At least take my slicker," Art said. "It's bound to rain."

Art twisted in the saddle, untied his slicker, rode near, and handed it to her. She took it with a smile of thanks.

He helped her put it on over her cloth outfit.

"Don't want you getting sick," he said.

Then he backed his horse and tipped his hat.

"Good day, Miss Rosalie. And don't forget about our picnic."

Rosalie tried to be pleasant, but sharp. "It might not be safe with men getting shot."

"You'll be safe with me," Art said.

The five men turned their horses and rode north, the way they came. Lehman and Motry looked over their shoulders, then followed the others.

Wes sat straight in the saddle, watching them for some time. When they were long gone from sight, he turned to Rosalie.

"You get on home."

"What was this about Lightning?"

"I'm telling you, go home."

"I'm going with you."

Wes was grim as he turned his horse to a zigzag pattern up

the side of the steep grade.

She followed, her smaller mare finding it more difficult.

It was starting to sprinkle, light but insistent.

Later the same day, Art, the Welsh brothers, Lehman, and Motry reined up on the spread of the north mesa. Rain was spreading dark across the Razorbacks to the east.

Art turned in the saddle; he could see no sign of Rosalie and Wes on the ridge. He pushed his hat back. “Lehman, you and Motry stick around.”

“They may not get back tonight,” Lehman said.

“If not, try again in the morning. I want Montana dead, but not in front of Rosalie.”

“How we gonna do that?”

“You’ll figure it out.” Art pulled his hat down tight. “And if they don’t come back, find something else to do.”

Lehman and Motry nodded, turned their horses, and rode back.

Clem was sweating. “Wes Montana. Who knew he’d show up here? Do you think he knows what we done?”

“Nobody knows,” Art said, “so keep your mouth shut.”

“But why is he here?”

“I said don’t worry about it.”

Late in the day, Art and the Welsh brothers rode up to the corrals of the Rodecker ranch. The barn and bunkhouse were well-built and -maintained. The place was impressive, with a fine sweep of the surrounding hills and distant cattle. Fine horses were being trained in the corral by three men.

The storm still hovered over the distant mountains.

The impressive white house with the wraparound porch had the appearance of the old South. Roses bloomed at the picket fence. On the porch, Pete Rodecker, sixty, a rough-looking but handsome man with a thin mustache, watched the corral as the men moved the horses into the barn.

He was sipping the last of his coffee. Pete was a taker. He never gave anything back.

Pete's philosophy was that the world was his. Anyone who got in his way was going to be sorry. He was feeling particularly good this morning.

His housekeeper and cook was part of his daily pleasure. Except he couldn't get near her and had to accept that or lose her skills in the kitchen. His belly, therefore, came first.

Anna Gomez, a pretty Mexican widow in her forties, came onto the porch and accepted his empty cup. A little plump but very beautiful, she was wearing an apron over her plain clothes. Her thick black hair was held back from her face, all the more showing her large dark eyes.

"You're a mighty fine cook," he said.

He smiled at her. She nodded her thanks, didn't smile back, and hurried inside again. He looked amused at how she avoided him. He took a cigar from inside his vest.

He knew he would never get anywhere near Anna, but she sure was all woman.

But Pete had other things on his mind. He was ambitious, greedy, willing to be as vicious as necessary to claim the entire mesa. He was still harboring anger that Eastman had jumped the land before him. The Utes had hardly left when Eastman had blown open a trail and headed his herd onto the tall grass.

Pete had his own plans now. He was spruced up with his best shirt, coat, and hat. He had the same slick hair as his son but he was more dignified, polished. His eyes were dark blue with trimmed eyebrows. He had a cigar in his teeth.

His saddled bay stood at the hitching rail, tail to the wind. Pete watched his son, Art, riding up to the rail. Art dismounted as Pete walked down to meet him. He liked his son, but he also harbored resentment that Art was still young and full of life.

"Where you been, son?"

"On the south side. Met up with Rosalie and Wes Montana."

"They were together?"

"No, she was just following him around."

"She's spirited all right," Pete said, suddenly hesitant. "What about him?"

"Hard as nails. Eyes like none I've ever seen. Like he's measuring you for a pine box."

"He working for Eastman?"

Art shrugged. "I don't know."

"He's only one man."

"Maybe so, but he's spooky. Made me plenty nervous."

"What about Rosalie?"

"She went off with him, up into the Razorbacks."

Pete frowned. "That's not good."

"They get back down, Lehman and Motry will be waiting. They'll take care of Montana. But not face on."

"And not in front of Rosalie."

Art shook his head. "I don't see her warming up to me. Besides, I don't see it doing us much good. It's Mona who gets the ranch. And she's your job."

"Well, I have news for you. Just got a message from our contact in the lawyer's office. Seems Eastman's will was changed. It leaves Mona a lot of money and that's all. The ranch goes to Chuck and Rosalie, or the survivor. All we need is Rosalie."

"You'd kill Chuck?"

"We'd make it look good." Pete adjusted his hat. "Right now, I got to meet with Mona. Getting harder for her to get away from the house with Eastman crippled up."

"If she doesn't get the ranch, why bother?"

Pete grinned. "Why do you think?"

That afternoon the sun was warm, but wind was rising. The storm still hovered over the distant Razorbacks.

Mona, wearing a fancy outfit and a cape with a hood, drove her buggy, pulled by a sorrel mare, into the trees, down to a secluded spot by the creek. She had packages in the back of the buggy. She stepped down and adjusted her outfit.

Moving down by the creek, Mona worried about the coming winter. If Peter did not secure the mesa before the heavy rains, she'd have no excuse to go to town alone.

This was how they'd first met, almost a year ago. She smiled as she recalled the day she was driving back from town when he had appeared out of the trees and tipped his hat. He made her feel young and beautiful.

Eastman had been away a lot then with roundup, cattle drives, meetings with the army. But now he was in the way. Mona would do anything for a hug and a kiss from Peter. Anything to make her feel alive, not just a cook and housekeeper and mother and often ignored wife.

She liked turning back the clock with Peter Rodecker. Today, she felt beautiful.

After striking different poses, she decided to sit on a rock, legs crossed. She heard a rider coming. She tilted her head sideways to see Pete riding through the trees. He looked wonderful. He dismounted, left his horse ground-tied, and walked down to the creek.

Striking her pose, she smiled at him.

Pete tipped his hat, walked over, took her hand, and pulled her to her feet.

"Mona, you're more beautiful by the day."

She moved into his arms. They kissed passionately.

Mona leaned back. "If you only knew how much it means to me, seeing you, alone out here. It's an escape, away from a beast of a man and that girl."

"And your son?"

"I can handle Charles."

She straightened in his arms, looking worried.

"Peter, he's here. Wes Montana is here."

"So I heard."

"If Ray learns who he is—"

"He doesn't know?"

"Montana hasn't told him. For some reason, he's toying with Ray."

"Don't worry," Pete said. "If it comes up, say that Montana tried to get money out of you, that it was all a lie."

"Why didn't they get rid of him at the same time?"

"Didn't know where he was."

"Or were afraid of him?"

Pete shrugged, not wanting to consider that possibility.

"I'll be so glad when the ranch is mine," Mona said. "When I've worn black long enough, we'll have a grand wedding."

"We'll have the whole mesa," he said.

They walked with his arm around her.

"Montana was seen riding with Rosalie," he said.

"What?"

Pete stood with his arms around her.

She was frustrated. "That girl!"

"They were going into the Razorbacks."

"Oh, no, then I'd better get home and tell Ray."

"And tell him how you knew?"

"No, no, I can't. But if she doesn't come back, they will look for her."

"And when they find her?"

Mona smirked. "If she's gone overnight, maybe Ray will stop

seeing her as some kind of princess."

They fell into a passionate embrace.

Late in the day, Rosalie and Wes were on the ridge and a perilous path. She had trouble keeping up with him. Wes had donned his slicker as it began to rain.

Art's slicker protected her clothing, but rain poured off her hat. And Wes's.

The rain was heavier as they rode. There was no wind. It was colder by the minute.

Far below and behind them was the grand mesa. The sun was already sinking in the west. Ahead of them, to the east, rose the white-crested Razorbacks.

"The rain will wash away our tracks," she said. "We'll be lost forever."

She smiled, but Wes was not amused.

"You can still go back," he said.

"I'm staying with you." She hesitated. "Do you know where we're going?"

Wes did not answer. He wasn't sure. They rode in all directions. The rain lessened to a drizzle.

Creaking leather, hooves hitting rock, and raindrops were the only sounds in the stillness. The air was clean, cold, scented with pine.

The view of the mesa below and beyond was still spectacular. They saw the ponds, indigo blue in the sun, only on Eastman's side. The horizon in the west was sprinkled with red cliffs.

Rosalie was thrilled whenever they stopped to look back.

"Ray says Utah has great red canyons with high cliffs," she said. "As if the good Lord had carved them out."

They turned and kept riding. Rain was off and on. It was late in the day. She was wet, cold, and miserable.

Wes could see she was weary and barely able to keep riding,

yet she never let on.

Wes dismounted as if to rest his horse and loosened the cinch. Rosalie sat her sidesaddle, hesitant. Then she rode close to a rock and stepped down. Weary, she moved around, keeping the reins in hand.

She made a face. "You can't believe how miserable it is to sit a sidesaddle. Bet some man dreamed it up. Says we can't have babies if we ride like men. I think they're afraid we'll outride them."

Wes was not used to being around such a forward woman. She was not blushing. He was, but hid it.

Rosalie gazed at the spectacular view but was worried.

"Shouldn't we be turning back?"

"Go ahead."

"It's too steep. And now it's muddy. I'd be afraid without you. I insist you go back with me."

Wes shook his head, gazing down at the mesa.

"I can't go alone," Rosalie said. "The trail is too dangerous. And I certainly can't stay a night up here."

"Walk your horse down."

"You're a crude and ruthless man. You must take me home."

Wes began to see her as comical. He tried to keep a straight face. She became all the more furious. "How dare you treat me this way!"

Wes looked away.

She fumed. "You are making me very angry."

Wes refused to look at her. He turned his back, his slight smile cracking a face that hadn't smiled in many a year.

Rosalie postured, hands on hips.

"Are you laughing at me?"

He turned, his lips tight but almost hinting at a smile.

"You beast."

He sobered, adjusted his hat, took up the reins, moved to

tighten the cinch. He dropped the stirrup. His buckskin nuzzled him.

Rosalie, angry, hot-faced, glared at him.

But she began to feel foolish. She giggled. With a sigh, she got up on the rock, drew her mount close, and climbed onto the sidesaddle.

She made a face. "I got myself into this, didn't I? Stubborn and bullheaded, that's me."

Wes mounted his horse. He tried not to laugh.

"I sure got myself in a fix." Shook her head. "Don't you ever talk? Why are you up here anyway?"

"To find Jedidiah."

"The hermit? They say he doesn't talk either. A fine pair you'll be." She was resigned. "Well, he'll have to be our chaperone."

Wes hid his amusement, and led the way.

It had been a long hard ride, but sharing it with a beautiful, spicy young woman had turned it into an adventure. That was something new to Wes. His life had been hard, rocky, bitter, and dangerous. There had been no time for anything but fighting his way through life.

But he knew he could never have this woman in his life. And why would she even look at a half-breed? So he accepted the adventure as a pleasant diversion.

Chapter Five

Toward evening as Wes and Rosalie rode into the forest facing the white capped Razorbacks, the rain became dark and persistent. They had been riding in every direction, searching.

But of a sudden, Wes spotted the needle rock, tall against the blackening sky. They rode into the forest and came to a small clearing where a log cabin was nestled, hidden in part by boulders. It had a chimney but no smoke. It was about as lonely as a place could be.

And silent but for the rain.

Wes dismounted and led his buckskin to an open-front shed in a small corral. There was a covered grain barrel in the shed and other gear. Rosalie dismounted by stepping on a rock and then she followed him, leading the bay mare into the corral.

They unsaddled, grained their mounts, and left them in the shelter of the shed. An old, carved-out log in the middle of the corral served as a watering trough and was full.

Night had come with the storm. Rain was heavy, following them. Wes led the way back to the cabin.

Inside Jedidiah's cabin, they lit lamps as rain and hail pounded the roof. Rosalie was shivering as she removed her slicker.

Wes removed his and hooked both on the wall.

Rosalie shook rain from her hat and hung it on the back of a chair. She sat down on the chair, exhausted.

The front part of the one-room cabin was cluttered with furs, gear, and traps. There were two bunks, one on either side of the room. The table and chairs were handmade.

Pine wood was stacked near the hearth. Walls were covered with hides. An old, smelly buffalo robe warmed the floor. Front and rear windows were shuttered from inside. There was oil paper that covered most of the walls and rifle slots on all sides.

The hail was loud on the roof. Rosalie shivered.

Wes started a fire in the stone hearth. Pitch from the pine sparked and crackled.

Rosalie huddled close to the flames and tried to warm herself. She knelt in front of it.

She frowned. "Where is he?"

"With his traps."

"But Ray said there was no money in furs. Not anymore. So why does he live like this?"

"Maybe to get away from women."

"You'd probably like it here."

Wes nodded as he prepared and put the coffee pot on a hook over the hearth fire.

He dangled a pot of beans over the other hook.

She sat back. "Some people have to live this way to be alone. You do it all by yourself."

Wes did not answer.

She watched him. "Why do you hate everybody? You must be the loneliest man in the West."

Wes tried to ignore her comments, but they hit hard.

She didn't know he was half Arapaho. He wondered what she would say. Maybe there would be that same disdainful look that had followed him all his life. He wasn't sure he could bear it, coming from her.

He gestured. "You can have the bunk closest to the fire."

She nodded her head and smiled. "Ray will be angry. But he's a pussycat. I can handle him. He gives me anything I want."

Pointedly. "He'd kill anyone who touched me."

Wes shrugged away her comments. Rosalie warmed her hands, and continued.

"But Mona hated it when he brought me to the ranch. Sent me right off to school." She laughed painfully. "I made sure they kept sending me home."

Wes didn't answer, but he could see she was hurting.

"It was different with my parents," she said. "They gave me a lot of love. My father was injured working on the railroad, so he bought a farm in Missouri. When I was sixteen, they died of some terrible sickness. It was so bad, the doctor had everything burned. All I could save was her music box. And the farm went for taxes."

Rosalie took a long moment, then continued. "I thought I would curl up and die, but neighbors took me in, and when more letters came from Ray, they let him know I was in trouble. He sent for me."

Rosalie took a minute to recover, then turned to him.

"What about your folks?"

Wes didn't answer, avoided her gaze.

"Maybe you didn't have any," she said.

Again, Wes didn't look at her, and she felt bad. "I'm sorry," she said softly. Her words echoed in the silence that followed.

Later, after they had eaten, Rosalie moved to one of the bunks, sat on it, loosened the laces on her boots, then stuck them out for removal and gazed at Wes.

Reluctantly, he went down on one knee in front of her to pull off her boots. As he did the first one, she smiled.

"That's right where I want you, Wes Montana."

He yanked her other boot so hard she slid off the bunk and landed with a thud on her rump. She gasped.

Wes stood, tossed the boot back at her. She caught it, glared at him, and rose off the floor.

"If Ray saw that, he'd shoot you dead."

She sat on the bunk, still angry. She lay back and pulled the blanket over her.

Wes took the other bunk, laying back with six-gun in hand.

The hail had stopped. They could barely hear the rain. The fire crackled and spit flames. She tossed and turned, then gazed at him. He could see she was having a difficult time of it.

"I can't sleep without my mother's music box." She sat up, laid down, turned again.

"I have bad dreams without it," she said.

Rolling about, she fought her blankets, and sat up.

"Could you play something?"

Wes sat up; he understood all too well. He took out his harmonica, tapped it in his hand. In the silence of the mountains and with only the crackle of the fire, he began to play softly.

The music was pleasing. She closed her eyes to listen. Wes played "Red River Valley" more than once.

He wondered, was he playing it for her comfort? Or was it in him to court her with the soft melody? All the while knowing that if she learned he was a breed, she would look down on him, scorn him?

When he rested a moment, she spoke with her eyes closed.

"You play 'Red River Valley' a lot," she said.

"It was my mother's favorite."

She fell asleep before he could say any more.

Wes stopped playing and gazed at her a long while. How any man would love to dig his fingers in all that shining red hair. Touch her pink cheeks where a few freckles danced. But Wes believed he would never have that chance, and it was painful.

He pocketed the harmonica and lay back down.

That same night, a lamp burned on the porch of the Eastman ranch house. Stars were sprinkling the black sky. Ray Eastman, on crutches, along with Mona and Chuck, stood on the porch.

They watched Jones and six men ride in and over to the corral. The men looked weary. Jones reined about, seeing them on the porch. He rode over to Eastman.

Shorty hesitated, then rode over to rein up beside him.

Jones leaned on the pommel. "As soon as it's daylight, we'll go back out. The only tracks we saw were run over by the cattle. But it ain't likely she went up into the Razorbacks. There ain't no real way to get up there."

"Jedidiah gets up there," Shorty said.

"He's like a mountain goat. She ain't," Jones said.

"I'd bet on Montana finding a way," Shorty added.

Jones, annoyed with Shorty, straightened. "Never should have told her where he was headed."

Mona hid her pleasure. "She's a headstrong girl. If they made it to that old hermit's cabin, they'll be all night."

"Yes, ma'am," Jones said, "but if she's with Montana, she'll be safe. I'd bet my life on it."

Eastman nodded. "You'll be doing that, all right."

Jones and Shorty turned and rode over to the corrals.

Chuck adjusted his hat. "I'm going with 'em."

"No, you're not," Mona said.

Eastman grunted. "Let the boy go."

Chuck looked pleased at his father's permission.

Mona angrily deferred to her husband.

That same night, up in the Razorbacks at Jedidiah's cabin, Wes lay asleep with six-gun in hand, resting on his chest. He could wake at the slightest sound.

Rain and wind returned and pounded the roof and walls. It sometimes whined and Wes awakened several times.

The door was barred from the inside, but in the mountains, there was no telling of intruders. Rosalie slept soundly in her bunk.

★ ★ ★ ★ ★

At daybreak, the rain and wind had stopped. Sunlight flashed at cracks in the windows.

Wes awakened at a tapping on the front door. Rosalie didn't stir.

Wes sat up and wearily looked around. He got up, gun in hand, went to a front window, and slid open the shutter. Satisfied, he closed the shutter and holstered his weapon.

He walked over and unbarred the door, then opened it.

Jedidiah, now in his mid-fifties, with long, graying brown hair but a clean-shaven face, entered. He wore buckskins and carried a long rifle. He looked like a cagey mountain man wary of civilization and living as the Indian, off the land. He gave the appearance of a man who'd kill you with his bare hands, if it came to that, or carry you on his back if you were bad hurt.

Every moment Jedidiah had ever spent trapping, hunting, braving the land was all in his gaze and every movement. It was like seeing history moving around the cabin.

Jedidiah looked Wes over, grunted.

As Wes closed and barred the door, Jedidiah stared at the sleeping Rosalie.

Wes followed his gaze. She looked more than beautiful, long red hair tossed about her face and throat.

Wes shook hands with Jedidiah. They spoke quietly.

"I'm Wes Montana."

"I'll be."

Wes nodded at Rosalie. "Rosalie Riley. She's living at the Eastman ranch."

"I've seen her afore. She rides like a wild Comanche."

Jedidiah put his rifle on a wall rack. He went to the low-burning fire and put in a chunk of wood. He shook the coffee pot, which still dangled over the now-crackling fire and was hot.

He served himself a cup of coffee and one for Wes. They sat at the table.

"How'd you find my place?"

"Bates. He told me about the needle rock."

"Forgot about that. Only time I shot my mouth off. But it don't matter none. And I'm glad you got here in time. I'm heading north for Blackfeet country as soon as I can pack up."

Jedidiah hesitated, then told the story.

"Way back afore I found your ma in the Medicine Bows, I was a young fella up in Montana Territory, over in the northwest. The woman I wanted to marry was a Blackfoot, but she was forced to marry in the tribe. Now I get a letter from an old trapper friend, saying as how she's a widow and is waiting for me. So I'm packing up."

"Sounds good."

"Yeah, I'm a nervous wreck." Jedidiah paused, studied Wes. "Last I saw, you was pan-size. How old are you now?"

"Twenty-four."

Jedidiah paused to sip his coffee.

Wes leaned back. "I'm grateful for what you did for my mother."

"Any man would have done the same."

Rosalie turned over; she appeared to be asleep.

Wes got up to kick a burning limb back into the fire. He came back to sit, savor his coffee. He wasn't sure how to handle the issue of his father.

But Jedidiah was glad to see Wes and liked him.

"I figure I know why you came up here. But why'd you bring the girl? Eastman will have a posse after you."

"Followed me. Wouldn't go back. Stubborn."

Jedidiah smiled at the sleeping Rosalie. "She's about as beautiful as they come."

"Yeah, and she knows it."

Jedidiah grinned. "Maybe so."

"I need to talk with you alone."

"The girl's asleep."

"I don't trust her. She'd blab everything. And I figure she's listening right now."

Rosalie, angered, sat up. She rubbed her eyes. "I am not."

Wes stayed sober, but Jedidiah grinned at her.

She got up and pulled on her boots. Stumbling over to the fire, she poured herself some coffee. She joined them at the table.

"I won't tell anyone. Whatever it is."

Wes turned to Jedidiah. "I can say this much. My mother was murdered by three men who got away. Three months ago. No proof who they was. She's buried at the Claymore ranch."

Rosalie saddened. "Wes, I'm sorry."

Jedidiah was deeply distressed. He took a long moment as he stared into his coffee. He spoke with a hushed voice.

"I didn't know. She was a real lady, Wes." They sat in an awkward silence.

Rosalie stood up, looked around. "Where's your necessary?"

"Outside. To your right."

Rosalie pulled on her coat. "Really, Mr. Jedidiah. I don't even see a chamber pot. What do you do in winter?"

"You don't want to know." She made a face, pulling her coat tight about her.

She went to the door, removed the bar, walked outside, and closed the door behind her.

Wes gazed at the closed door but didn't smile.

"You like that girl," Jedidiah said.

"Yeah, she's a real kick."

"I'm sorry about your ma."

"I wasn't much of a son." Wes moved to kneel at the hearth and stoke the fire. The hot pitch spat at him.

Jedidiah watched Wes, and liked him more every minute.

Wes poked the wood in place. "You wrote her about Eastman."

"Yes," Jedidiah said, "and I worried over telling her."

Wes was grim, eyes gleaming as he stood. "When she got the news from you, she wrote Ray Eastman, told him about us, even gave my name as Wes Montana, and not long after that, she was murdered. If I hadn't been up in Wyoming Territory, they would have tried to get me as well. And now . . ."

"What are you thinking, Wes?"

"I figure Ray Eastman had something to do with her death." Wes returned to his chair. "I had it in mind to kill him."

"What stopped you?"

"He's like an old grizzly."

"He's a man's man, all right." Jedidiah agreed. "Only saw him a couple times when I was trading in town. Everyone got out of his way, that's for sure."

Wes fingered his cup. "He could have paid someone to get rid of her."

"You figure he could do a thing like that?"

"He left her to die in the snow, afore I was born."

"You can't be sure. It was one devil of a storm. Wiped out the whole Arapaho camp. Your mother only survived because she had some food and made a snow cave."

"You found her. Why didn't he?"

Jedidiah paused to scratch. Scratched again.

"I don't know, but that was the worst blizzard ever hit the Medicine Bows. Your pa had good reason to figure she was dead."

"Don't make excuses for him."

Jedidiah got up, poured himself some more coffee. Brought the pot to refill Wes's cup.

"Your ma was a good-looking woman." Jedidiah returned the

pot, then sat down. "I figured she'd marry down on the flats."

Wes stood up. "Would have been better for us."

"And maybe you wouldn't have turned into a gun hand?" Jedidiah shook his head. "Every man makes his own way, Wes. You would have been the same. It was in you to fight the whole world."

"I reckon you're right."

"Now tell me more about Eastman."

"He didn't seem to believe me when I said she was murdered three months ago. I didn't expect that. He claimed he never got no letter from her."

"So you're not leaving?"

"I was thinking that, but now I figure to stick around and get some answers." He lightened up. "And I got myself a half brother. I might want to know him better."

"And the girl?"

"She's the granddaughter of Bob Riley, the man who went trapping with Eastman, just before that blizzard. Said Riley saved Eastman's life, but she doesn't know any more than that, and Riley's dead a long time back. And she lost her own folks, who might have known a little more."

"Your mother spoke about Riley, but that's the first I ever heard of him or your pa. And if either of 'em was ever at a rendezvous, I wouldn't have known who they was. Not with all the goings-on."

"I always thought my father's name was Montana."

"That was to protect you, in case he had kinfolk who might come and take you away from her."

"So I was told."

Jedidiah hesitated. "You going to tell him who you are?"

Wes filled their cups, then took the pot back to the hearth. He sat down again. It took a while to answer.

"Not yet."

"Whatever happens, you get rid of the hate, you'll be a better man for it."

"Only one way to get rid of it."

"Kill Eastman?"

Wes looked away, nodded. "He had good reason. Got himself a new life. Not wanting some Arapaho woman to show up and cause him shame."

"You can't be sure."

"He done it all right."

"Listen to me, Wes, you may never find out who was to blame. What then?"

"I don't know."

The door opened as Rosalie returned from the cold.

The men fell silent as she closed the door behind her. Rosalie looked them over.

"Okay, what's the big secret now?"

"We were talking about you." Jedidiah said.

"Nicely, I hope."

Wes looked stern. "I was telling Jedidiah what a brat you are."

She made a face. Jedidiah smiled. She smiled back.

She looked at the sober Wes. "Mr. Jedidiah, what do you think of a man who never smiles?"

Jedidiah grinned at her and Wes. "It would crack his face."

Wes said nothing but sipped his coffee.

Her chin went up. "Everybody's afraid of him, but I'm not."

"No," Jedidiah said, "I can see that."

Rosalie ignored them as she went to warm herself at the hearth.

It was late morning at Jedidiah's.

The sky was clearing but it was still cold. Wes and Rosalie were outside and ready to leave. Rosalie was in the saddle, already some distance away but restraining her mare. She was waiting impatiently, out of earshot.

Over in the corral, a mule and saddle horse were waiting for Jedidiah.

Wes stood in front of the cabin, reins in hand, talking to Jedidiah. Wes turned to look at Rosalie. Her red hair was blowing around her face.

"Ravishing," Jedidiah said. "What are you waiting for?"

"She's not for me."

"Girl like that, she chooses a fella, right then she stops being particular." He grinned. "And he won't have a thing to say about it."

"It won't be me."

"You mean, because you're half Arapaho. Well, don't sell her short, son."

"Not her. Everyone else."

"You don't have it easy, I'll grant you that."

Wes reached to shake Jedidiah's hand. "Thanks for everything," he said.

"You be careful, Wes, and remember, sometimes, things ain't what they seem."

"Or maybe they are." Wes mounted his horse.

"You need me, head for Blackfoot Country."

"No, you just enjoy your new life."

"That I will." Jedidiah said. "I've been waiting near thirty years for her." He frowned. "If she still likes what she sees."

"She will."

Jedidiah nodded, grinned. "Yes, sir."

"And so will you."

Jedidiah seemed to float.

By late afternoon in the warm sun, Rosalie and Wes had left the high country and storm behind them. They were working their way down the dangerous trail toward the dry mesa far below.

At one point, they were side by side. She glanced at him. "So, did you like Jedidiah?"

Wes nodded and led the way. She tried to keep up. Wes kept riding. She managed to come alongside.

"I hope he has a happy marriage. Except he's probably just like you."

"What does that mean?"

"I'm not going to tell you, Wes Montana."

"Figures." Wes twisted in the saddle to look back, saw the dark clouds still stuck over the Razorbacks.

They reached the foot of the trail in bright sunshine and were on the mesa when they reined up. There were no signs of any searchers. Gunfire echoed in the hills to the south of them.

Wes was alert, looking around. No sign of anyone.

"Head for home. Now," he said.

"I will not."

"Do as I say."

"I'm staying right here."

"Then get over in the trees and stay put."

She hesitated, then turned her mare.

"I don't come back, you head for the ranch."

Rosalie rode out of sight into the trees.

More gunfire.

Wes drew his Winchester from the scabbard and rode south into the hills.

Rosalie peered out, worried.

Wes rode through the trees, his Winchester in hand. More gunfire.

Wes stepped down from the saddle, then moved on foot through the rocks and trees. He soon came on a view of the rocky canyon below and started down to that level.

One Eastman hand, old Tom, lay dead, flat on his back.

Another Eastman hand, Travers, an old-timer, was in the rocks, firing his rifle across the canyon.

Wes didn't know Travers but he could see Lehman and Motry on the other side.

Travers had to be an Eastman hand.

Their horses had trotted off down the canyon and stopped.

At the far side opposite and facing Travers, Lehman and Motry were entrenched and firing. Their horses were in the trees behind them, at the canyon wall.

Travers, fallen out of sight, stopped shooting.

A long moment of silence. Lehman and Motry rose up, six-guns in hand.

"Hey, Travers, you dead?" Lehman shouted.

No answer.

Lehman and Motry were grinning as they crossed the canyon floor on foot. They held their revolvers ready.

"Hold it," Wes said, stepping out of the trees.

Lehman and Motry spun, both firing at the same time.

Wes dived as he fired and hit Lehman.

Travers rose up with his rifle and shot Motry dead center.

Lehman and Motry sprawled on the canyon floor, dead long before they could realize who they had just been up against.

Travers came out of the rocks, rifle in hand. He hurried to kneel by old Tom, but it was too late.

Wes made sure Motry and Lehman were dead.

Travers stood up. "We were out looking for you and Miss Rosalie. Everyone has."

"Catch up their horses," Wes said.

"What about them?"

"We'll send 'em back to Rodecker." In the canyon, it wasn't long before Motry and Lehman were tied over their saddles and sent on their way.

Travers and Wes put old Tom across his own saddle. They

covered him with a blanket and tied him in place.

North of the canyon, in the trees, Rosalie waited, impatient.

Then she saw two horses coming into the open with Lehman and Motry across their saddles. She rode out of the trees to watch their mounts carry them north toward the Rodecker ranch and home.

She turned to see Wes and Travers, who was leading old Tom's horse with Tom over the saddle, covered with a blanket. They rode into the open.

"Mr. Travers," she said, riding forward.

"Sorry, Miss Rosalie. We lost old Tom."

"I'm so sorry," she said. "What were you doing out here?"

"Looking for you."

Rosalie was stricken.

Travers, appearing heartbroken, turned his horse and rode toward the Eastman ranch, leading his friend's horse with Tom across the saddle.

Her eyes wet, Rosalie watched them out of sight. Then she turned to look at Wes. "They've been together a long time," she said. "Thank you for saving Mr. Travers."

He could see her thanks were genuine. He tipped his hat and turned his buckskin. She wiped at her eyes, fighting for calm. It had been years since she had been able to cry, and she was hurting from it.

She rode behind Wes as her tears streamed. She was crying for Tom and Travers. She was crying for Wes's mother. Tears fell as even her own mother and father came into her thoughts. And she was letting go for all her own misery with Mona. She wiped at her eyes and stayed back until her tears diminished.

Wes knew she was crying. That was something he couldn't handle. At length, she was in control. No more tears. She wiped her eyes again and caught up with him.

She and Wes rode side by side in silence.

Wes could not look at her out of fear of seeing just one tear.

It reminded him, painfully, of how one tear in his mother's eye had been unbearable. All the more painful for knowing how she had died.

Rosalie kept silent.

Wes looked back from time to time at the dark clouds remaining over the Razorbacks. He, too, had nothing to say.

Her tears reflected all his pent-up anger and rage. He accepted she was crying for both of them. It eased his aching heart and the anger still boiling inside him.

A short while later, on the mesa, in the open, Rosalie and Wes reined up. Coming toward them were Sam Jones and Chuck.

Wes and Rosalie rested their horses. The riders charged toward them. They reined up short.

Chuck was at first delighted, then angry.

"We just saw Travers," Jones said to Wes. "He said you saved his hide. Sent the killers on home, tied to their saddles. But he's pretty broke up about old Tom."

Chuck ignored Wes's having saved Travers. "Rosalie, you know better than to ride off like that. You were gone all night. We hunted the whole mesa."

Rosalie's chin went up. "We went to Jedidiah's. It was too late to come back. And I was well-chaperoned, thank you."

Chuck grimaced. "You go with Mr. Jones. I want to speak with Montana."

"Now, Chuck, it was all my fault. I followed him. But the trail was too dangerous for me to come back alone."

"Just do as I tell you."

"I will not. If you have anything to say to Mr. Montana, I want to hear it."

Chuck glared at Wes.

"Montana, you stay away from Rosalie. You ain't wanted

around here."

Rosalie giggled. "Chuck, you sound just like Ray. All growl and no bite."

Jones remained calm. "Let's think about it, Chuck. The Rodeckers are getting braver. We lost another dozen head of cattle. Three of our men was run off and never came back. Two of our hands was found shot full of holes a couple weeks ago. And now we done lost old Tom. If it hadn't been for Wes, we would have lost Travers."

Chuck wasn't about to bend.

"We don't know if those boys were following orders," Chuck said.

"They work for Rodecker," Jones replied. "And your pa already asked me to hire Wes, if he's a mind."

"We don't need him," Chuck said.

"How so?"

"Rosalie's going to marry Art and make the peace."

Her chin shot up. "I am not."

She rode on ahead, nose in the air.

Jones stayed to keep things under control between Chuck and Wes. He hid his own amusement. Chuck worked his jaw. He studied Wes.

"Let's get this straight, Montana. I don't like your looks. I figure you shot a few men in cold blood and never batted an eye." Chuck tugged at his hat brim. "So from now on, I catch you around Rosalie, you'll have to answer to me."

Wes swallowed his amusement. He was proud of this feisty young half brother, enjoyed the bravado, especially when stronger, hardier men shook in their boots around Wes.

Filled with anger and self-importance, Chuck turned his horse to follow Rosalie.

Wes and Jones watched them ride away. Jones grunted.

"Don't you worry, son. We're going to need a man like you."

"He's right about one thing. I got no business around her."

"Nothing between Chuck and Rosalie. He's just protective. Besides he's still a kid." He grinned. "Too young to be afraid of Wes Montana."

Wes nodded, deep in admiration for his young half brother.

Chuck was full of bravado and had showed no fear in the face of a known gunfighter. But not a sign of good sense.

"Now then," Jones said, "I figure you'll want more than forty a month and grub, so what's your going rate?"

"To work for Ray Eastman?"

Jones nodded, waiting as Wes chewed on it. "I don't want his money."

"You don't want to work for him?"

"I'll work for you, but not for pay."

Jones was bewildered. "I don't get it."

"You tell him I'm taking the forty, but I don't want it."

"How can I make him believe it? A famous gun like you?"

"Aren't you the foreman?"

"Yeah, but . . . let's do this. If he asks, I'll just say a thousand when the fight's over, if you're still alive."

Wes nodded agreement.

Chapter Six

When they reached the Eastman ranch that night, Wes, Rosalie, Chuck, and Jones glanced toward the porch where lamps were burning. The air was cold and damp. Stars were shining.

Mona and Eastman came out of the house. Eastman hobbled onto the porch on his crutches. Mona appeared to help him. They were waiting to lay the hammer on Rosalie and Wes. Wes and Jones reined up at the corrals as Chuck and Rosalie rode ahead to the house.

Chuck straightened in the saddle, turned to Rosalie. "Now you're in for it."

Rosalie shrugged, trying to develop her defense.

Jones and Wes dismounted and left their horses at the corral. They walked toward the house, where Rosalie and Chuck were still in the saddle at the picket fence.

The yellow dog trotted over, growled at Jones but fell into step with Wes.

Jones grunted. "Except for Ray, you're the only one that dog likes. Are you kin?"

"No, but I had a pup like him. Once."

Wes swallowed hard, remembering the pup he had given his mother, the little dog that had died with her. Nothing in this life was going to be easy for Wes, not anymore.

At the picket fence, Chuck dismounted under his parents' glare, then went around to help Rosalie swing down.

Wes and Jones were approaching, slowly.

Rosalie walked over to and up the steps, onto the porch, and kissed Eastman on the cheek. She acted as if she had only been gone for a few hours.

Mona was angry. "Young lady, you're in a lot of trouble."

"I was properly chaperoned," Rosalie smiled. "The view was wonderful. We could see for miles in every direction. At one spot, we could see the red hills of Utah."

"And more men are dead," Mona said, glaring toward Wes.

"Wes saved Mr. Travers," Rosalie said.

Ray Eastman glared at Wes.

"Montana, you get over here."

Wes walked through the gate with Jones. He walked up the steps and onto the porch so he didn't have to look up.

Wes and Eastman, on crutches, stood eye to eye as Rosalie joined them.

Eastman's voice was barely contained. "What right you got, keeping Rosalie out all night?"

Wes was silent, refusing to back down.

Rosalie laughed. "He tried to send me back," Rosalie said. "I insisted on going because no one ever let me ride up there. It was my only chance to see it. And Jedidiah's cabin."

"What on earth for?" Mona asked.

Eastman understood. It softened his anger, but he still chastised her. "Girl, you need a talking to."

Rosalie was contrite. "I'm terribly sorry about Old Tom, but I'm glad we went. Jedidiah's going away to live with the Blackfeet Indians, way up north. He's got himself a girlfriend up there."

"Good for him," Eastman said.

Rosalie moved over to Eastman and kissed his cheek again.

Eastman grimaced. "Chuck, you go inside with your mother. You, too, Rosalie. I want to talk with Montana."

Jones, taking the hint, turned back and led the horses away to the corral.

Chuck and Mona went inside.

Rosalie studied Wes, then Eastman.

"Wes, don't be afraid of him. He's a puppy dog."

Eastman glowered. "Get inside, and I don't want nobody hanging their ear at that there window."

Rosalie smiled, kissed Ray's cheek, and went inside, closing the door behind her.

Eastman staggered over to a bench, away from the door and window, and sat down.

Wes moved over to stand near him.

The night was cold and dark.

"Montana, we got to talk."

"She was safe the whole time."

"I know that. I trust her more'n the likes of you." Deep breath. "First off, thank you for saving Travers. Did Jones hire you on?"

Wes nodded, but Eastman had more on his mind than Wes's pay and didn't question whatever Jones had offered. He was more interested in attacking Wes's story.

"Good," Eastman said. "Now, you tell me about this Claymore. And his lie about Mary Antelope."

"He gave me the message before he died. Just doing him a favor."

"What game was he playing?"

Wes was evasive. He didn't want to tell this man anything.

"You knew her?"

Wes shrugged, shook his head, forced to lie. Eastman glared at him.

"You see her body?"

"No. He showed me her grave, behind the house. Said she wrote a letter to you about three months ago."

"Mary didn't know how to read or write."

"Maybe he wrote it for her."

"How'd she even know I was alive?"

"He didn't say."

"How'd she end up at the Claymore ranch, all the way from—"

"I don't know. All he said was how she was living there. And not long after she mailed the letter she was murdered. Mr. Claymore asked me to bring the word."

Eastman took a long moment before responding.

"Mary Antelope and the whole Arapaho camp was wiped out in a blizzard early in fifty-nine, over in the Medicine Bows. More than twenty-odd years ago."

Wes remained silent, trying to read him.

"The camp was low on meat, so my partner Riley and I had gone hunting when the blizzards hit, one after another. We were trapped in a cave for weeks. When we got back to the camp, they was all dead and buried. The army said no one survived. I didn't want to believe 'em." He took a deep breath. "We rode all over them mountains, got lost, hit with an avalanche. We gave up after a few months and the snow was gone."

Wes wanted to believe Eastman, but he was still unsure.

"What was she to you?" Wes asked.

"She was my wife. Not a civil marriage. Or in no church. But it was a marriage, all right. There was the exchange of gifts, of horses, the marriage feast, and her brother's blessing. The whole tribe celebrated. I loved that woman. And when she was gone, when I couldn't find her, that was the closest I ever came to . . . but Riley stopped me."

Wes almost believed him.

Eastman paused, swallowed hard before asking. "Did she marry again?"

Wes shook his head. His own torment matched Eastman's.

He wanted to tell Eastman who he was. He had a terrible need to tell him.

But suppose Eastman was guilty and had been lying about never receiving the letter? Suppose it was one long story. Wes started to turn away.

Eastman growled. "Wait. How do I know what you're telling me is true?"

"It's what I was told."

"By a man who's dead."

Wes nodded, started to turn away again.

"And they never found who killed her?"

Wes shook his head, anxious to leave.

Eastman wasn't getting anywhere with his questions. He studied Wes, wasn't sure about him, but needed him.

"We'll let it go at that, but we want you to stay."

Wes hesitated as he looked at this grizzly of a man. Despite everything, he liked Ray Eastman. If a boy had to have chosen a father, this man would have been first choice. But what if he was guilty?

Wes nodded just the same. He would stay.

"Good," Eastman said. "One more thing, I'd like you to spend some time with Chuck. Maybe you can help him buckle down."

Wes nodded, turned, and went down the stairs, walking away toward the horses at the corral where Jones was waiting.

Eastman watched Wes to the corrals.

A terrible weight was on Eastman's shoulders. If the story was true, he had left Mary to die in the mountains. If it was true, the love he had shared had been shattered with no going back. And if true, she was dead a second time, brutally murdered. He felt terrible guilt. No return of the joy, the wonderful sharing with a woman the likes of whom he would never find again.

It was too much for him to accept. The only way to survive was to believe it was all a lie. That was better. It was all a dirty lie.

Eastman banged on the wall and Chuck came out to help Eastman into the doorway. Eastman peered back out the door.

Wes did not look back.

That same night, Ray Eastman, still dressed, sat on a chair in his bedroom, his leg propped up. He glared at Chuck, who had just pulled off his father's boots.

Chuck, fully dressed, stood with hat in hand.

Eastman looked as mean as ever.

"Pa, I don't trust him."

"I ask you to do one thing—"

"But we can do our own fighting."

"Just show him the ranch."

"Geez, Pa, you never trust my judgment."

"And you never do as you're told."

"I been busting my backside trying to please you since I was knee high, but you—"

"Listen, son—"

"First time you called me son in years."

"I've been hard on you, I know."

"All I want is to do things your way."

Eastman softened, nodded, then continued.

"I haven't told this to anyone, but some time ago, I changed my will. The ranch goes to you and Rosalie. Mona gets all the money she'll need to leave this place. She doesn't like it here. And the law can be tricky on a wife's inheritance when it comes to land. So it's better for her."

Chuck reacted with a surprised look. Half the ranch? Not under Mona's fist? Yes, a son should inherit from his father.

Chuck nodded. "Thanks, Pa."

"But I ain't in no hurry for you to collect."

Chuck grinned as did Ray, despite himself.

"Does Rosalie know?"

"Not yet. She might give it away to Mona."

Chuck pulled his hat down, savored Eastman's unexpected but temporary softness, turned and left for his room.

Early the next morning, Wes was alone at the corrals as the hands rode out. He leaned on the fence and stared at the house. He turned to look at the Razorbacks, where the black clouds still hovered. He saw a flash of lightning. But the mesa remained dry.

Wes was unsure about the turn of events. Ray Eastman wanted him to work with Chuck at the same time Wes was ready to kill Ray, the boy's father. Wes's father.

Wes reminded himself of the brutal death of his mother. He had come here for revenge. This day's ride changed nothing.

Chuck came out of the house, down the steps, and walked over to Wes.

Chuck was still plenty annoyed with his father's interest in Wes, but he would do anything to please Eastman. Especially now that he knew the ranch would someday belong to him and Rosalie, not to his mother, who was desperate to sell.

Chuck's only real irritation now was Wes Montana. Chuck pushed his hat back, unfriendly.

Wes watched his cocky half brother take a stance. Wes liked Chuck.

"Hey, Montana, I don't know what got into the old man, but I'm supposed to show you the ranch."

"I'm working for him."

"Yeah, I know." Chuck relented. "Well, come on, let's saddle up before Rosalie tags along."

★ ★ ★ ★ ★

Over the day, Chuck and Wes rode all over the mesa.

The black clouds still hovered over the Razorbacks, and Wes thought often of Jedidiah, the man who had saved his mother and was now on his way to the north country.

Chuck was suspicious of Wes, who had little to say.

They rode past one of the herds. Chuck gestured. "We got better stock than Rodecker, and he knows it. His scrubs have been trying to mix." Chuck spoke with amusement. "One of his bulls tangled with one of ours and went home with one horn dangling."

Wes rode along in silence.

"Trouble is," Chuck said, "we know who killed old Tom but not the other two we found dead. It's coming to a fight, real soon."

Wes didn't answer. He liked listening to Chuck's voice.

Later, Wes and Chuck rode into a grove of cottonwoods along a creek.

"Rodecker has some killers on his payroll," Chuck said. "I reckon that's why Pa hired you."

Wes didn't answer.

"If they're afraid of you, you'll get it in the back."

Wes didn't like that thought much, but he liked Chuck. Wes leaned over to stroke his horse's neck.

"But I'm not afraid of you," Chuck said, and added with a grin, "and neither is Rosalie."

Wes had to agree with him.

They dismounted, loosened the cinches, and tethered their horses. Wes took a canteen along as they walked near the water. Chuck fingered his holster, his six-gun.

"So how come you got your left gun butt forward?" Chuck asked.

"No good with my left hand."

"But you use the right pistol first?"

"Unless my coat's in the way. The left is easier to grab."

Chuck seemed satisfied and also impressed.

Wes hadn't figured out his half brother as yet. He watched him, liked him. It was comforting to have real kinfolk, even a seventeen-year-old kid who didn't know much about life beyond the spread.

But Wes was only twenty-four, and he realized this, except that he had aged threefold while hunting rustlers and having to kill more than one for the Cattlemen's Association. He hoped Chuck would never have to shoot a man.

Chuck got down near the creek, gestured to some tall trees.

"Every time I come down here, I pick off some of them little branches."

Chuck took a stance facing the trees, his back to Wes; he drew his six-gun, pulled the hammer, fired.

A small twig sailed off the high branches.

Chuck straightened, twirled his six-gun back into the holster. He turned around, looked full of it, grinned, gestured to Wes.

"You think you can do better?"

Wes shook his head.

Chuck came back up the incline and glared at Wes.

"You funning me?"

Wes shook his head, pushed his hat back.

"I'd be faster," Chuck said, "with one of them new double actions, but Pa won't buy 'em. And he won't say why."

Wes put his hand on his single-action Colt.

"Too easy," Wes said.

"Because?"

"The first shot is self-defense," Wes said. "The second is to finish the kill. A rush to judgment, but single action gives you time to think."

Chuck considered this, accepted it.

"Makes sense." Hesitated. "Let me see how fast you are."

Wes wasn't one to show off, but this was his kid brother.

Wes drew and fired, hit one of the twigs.

Chuck was astounded. "How'd you shoot so fast?"

Wes holstered his weapon, demonstrated.

"When you reach for it," Wes said, "have your thumb on the hammer, pull it back as your gun leaves the holster." Wes demonstrated again.

Chuck tried it, twice. The third time, he spun and fired, hit a twig that shot into the air. Chuck was delighted. They both reloaded.

Chuck sat on nearby rock and turned to watch the horses.

"I guess," Chuck said, "you never met a man faster'n you, or you wouldn't be here."

Wes did not respond, but sat on a rock, drank from his canteen, and handed it to Chuck, who sipped and returned it.

Wes capped the canteen and set it aside.

"You play your harmonica pretty good," Chuck said.

Wes did not volunteer to take it out and play.

Chuck grinned. "But I'd rather have me a guitar and sing. Girls like that. If I ever get to meet any." He shook his head. "Rosalie, we're just pals." Chuck stretched and yawned.

"Tell me about your pa," Wes said.

"All I can say is, I wish I was like him."

"Why?"

"He's tough, ornery, fights at the drop of a hat, honest, and he gets all soft and sissy when a colt is born." Chuck thought back. "And when I was a kid, he used to tell me stories about the old days. He traveled all over the Rockies and up to Canada, even."

Wes swallowed hard. "He ever married before?"

"I don't think so."

"What about when he was a trapper?"

Chuck yawned. "All I know is, Rosalie's grandpa was his partner. I guess they trapped up and down the Rockies when Pa was young. But they fought for the Union in the War. Riley got hit by a cannon ball, didn't live much longer after that. I guess Pa never got over it. That's why he was glad to take in Rosalie when she lost her folks."

"And your mother? How did they meet?"

"Pa was a captain. She was his sergeant's widow. About that time the War was ending. She wanted to be an officer's wife. So they got married."

"And?"

"Pa mustered out, and she had a fit. But he went to work around Denver for a big cattle company and then for the railroad and made a lot of money, so that made her happy enough. We had a big house and nice things."

"You were born there?"

"Yeah, in Denver. Ma wanted to stay there. You know, the opera and all that. Pa wanted his own spread, so here we are. It cost plenty to stock the place, and there wasn't much left for a fancy house, so that made a little trouble."

Wes wasn't sure he liked the picture being painted of Mona, but Eastman was looking more like a good man. A good man Wes might have to kill.

"What about your folks?" Chuck asked.

"Lost my mother a few months ago."

"Sorry. And your pa?"

"Never knew him."

"So how come you got to be a hired gun?"

"It came natural."

"And it pays good, huh?"

Wes nodded. "Enough to get my own spread."

"That why you come here?"

Wes shook his head, looked at Chuck with a good feeling.

They both stopped, listened. They heard hoofbeats and stood up.

Of a sudden, they both walked to their horses, tightened the cinches, and mounted.

The riders were coming closer.

Chuck squinted in the sun. "Ain't Rosalie. Ma's sitting on her today. Can't be the boys. Ain't none of 'em riding out this way."

Wes and Chuck rode to the edge of the grove of trees. They saw three riders coming at a lope. The riders slowed to a walk as they approached.

Chuck grimaced. "Kid Lightning. Miller. And ole crazy Potluck. You made fools of 'em and they ain't forgot it." He shook his head. "And they ain't drunk this time."

Kid Lightning, Miller, and Potluck were afraid of Wes but considered him outnumbered, as they gave no credence to seventeen-year-old Chuck.

They also had their revolvers already drawn, out of sight, but brought them up and aimed.

They slid their horses to a halt in front of Wes and Chuck.

Kid Lightning slowly smiled. "Well, what have we here?"

Miller sneered. "A couple of easy targets."

Kid Lightning motioned to Chuck and Wes. "You're on Rodecker land."

Chuck reacted. "My father owns the mesa. He lets Rodecker squat on the north half, so don't push it."

Kid Lightning straightened. "You got about one minute to get off this spread."

"Yeah," Miller said to Chuck, "You're in real trouble."

"You're asking for it," Chuck said.

Potluck grinned. "Hey, the kid has spunk."

Kid Lightning waved his revolver. "Let's finish it, here and now."

"Yeah," Miller said, "we ain't drunk this time."

Potluck was enjoying having the edge.

Wes looked deadly. "I don't figure you fellas can do anything without orders."

Kid Lightning stiffened. "Oh, yeah?"

Chuck took up the story. "Yeah."

Kid Lightning grimaced. "Oh, yeah?"

"Take it easy, Kid," said Potluck. "He's right."

Kid straightened. "Unless we're defending ourselves."

Miller nodded. "The way I see it, these here fellas pulled down on us."

Miller, Lightning, and Potluck brazenly kept their weapons on Wes and Chuck.

Potluck signaled to Chuck and Wes. "And if you don't slap leather, we're gonna rope and drag you halfway 'cross the mesa."

Chuck held to his bravado. Wes was silent, watching.

Kid Lightning looked ready. "So make your play."

Chuck and Wes did not move. Chuck seemed to read Wes's mind. Using a man as a target, that was a new thought to Chuck. But he knew he and Wes were in a lot of trouble.

He called on the bravado he saw in Wes.

Chuck said, "I'll take Potluck. The other two, they're yours."

Kid Lightning, Miller, and Potluck were overconfident. They snickered. Their eyes narrowed and flashing. They were ready to fire. They figured they had Wes and Chuck hands down.

Wes's hand moved so fast, it was a blur. He fired, fanned the hammer, fired again before the surprised Miller and Kid Lightning could react. Both were hit dead center, their eyes wide with horror.

Potluck was startled, distracted for a second.

Chuck drew fast, hit Potluck before the man could fire.

Potluck's gun fell to the ground as he grabbed his chest.

Miller and Kid Lightning were dead in the saddle. Their

horses spun around.

Miller fell, his boot caught in the stirrup. His horse moved away and stopped, looking back at the man dragging beside it.

Kid Lightning, even in death, clung to the saddle, then fell to the ground and rolled aside.

Potluck, unarmed, wounded, and clinging to the saddle, stared at the dead.

Wes and Chuck holstered their guns, dismounted, and tied the dead across their saddles, reins wrapped on the horns.

Chuck tried to stay calm and strong as he glared at Potluck. "You tell Rodecker to stay off our land."

In pain and shock, Potluck grimaced. "I'll tell 'em plenty."

Chuck glared at him. "You'd better say as how you throwed down on us. And it was a fair fight." He gestured. "Or we'll come looking for you, personal."

Potluck took up his reins. "This ain't the end of it."

Potluck turned north. The other horses followed when Chuck waved at them.

When Potluck and the dead were out of sight, Chuck fell apart.

"My God, I nearly killed him."

"You was just defending yourself."

"Yeah, you're right, but I got a rock in my gut."

Wes was silent as they reloaded. Chuck remained stunned. "This could start a war. You got to back me up with Pa." Chuck walked around, unable to grasp the shooting. "I never shot a man before. Deer, elk. But a man?"

Wes was calm. "Well, let's back up and say you didn't slap leather." He paused for effect. "Maybe we'd both be buzzard bait. I don't figure I could have taken all three." Wes shook his head. "But even if I did take 'em, you'd be all bloody and dead. I'd have to put you in the saddle, and you ain't that small."

Chuck was getting the message.

Wes continued. "I'd get your blood all over me. Be a real mess. Then I'd have to take you back. First off, your pa would be real mad and cuss me out. Your ma, she'd be crying." Wes adjusted his hat. "Your pal, Rosalie, she'd never speak to me again."

Chuck was starting to return to normal.

Wes adjusted his gun belt. "Potluck would be back at Rodecker's, bragging how they took us." He dusted his shirt. "And this is my only shirt. I'd never get your darn blood off it."

Chuck listened, forced himself to grin. "I bet that's the most you ever said at one time in your whole life."

Wes stayed sober but nodded.

Chuck showed bravado, adjusted his hat and gunbelt. They turned and walked over to their horses. Chuck bent over to pick up the fallen weapons.

Wes was feeling so close to his half brother, it hurt.

Suppose everything fell apart. Maybe Eastman had had Mary Antelope murdered. And Wes had to kill his own father. Wes would lose all connection with Chuck.

Chuck forced the three pistols into his belt. "Wait'll Pa sees this."

"I'd unload 'em first."

"Hey, you're right." Chuck grinned, took out the pistols, and ejected the shells.

"I could've ended up a girl," Chuck said.

Wes almost smiled.

As they caught up their horses and remounted, Wes was feeling a lot closer to Chuck.

"Pa's gonna be real surprised," Chuck said, beaming.

What a great kid, Wes thought. *The boy wants only to have a friend, to be liked, to be accepted, and to be really connected with family. I sure wish we'd grown up together, taking the whole world face on while he was laughing. How can I kill his pa? Our pa?*

That'll take a lot of doing. Maybe more than I got in me.

They turned back toward the ranch. The sun was high in the sky.

Sometimes, even for a minute, life was good.

Chapter Seven

In the late afternoon, Wes and Chuck rode in to the Eastman ranch and left their horses at the corral. Chuck was so full of himself, he was beaming.

Chuck had three six-guns stuck inside his belt. He held his hat in front of them as they walked over to the house. Wes was sober but enjoying Chuck.

The dog trotted over to greet Wes.

Rosalie and Ray Eastman were sitting on the porch bench. Rosalie stood and moved to the railing as they approached.

She looked particularly beautiful, her hair soft at her throat, wearing a blue dress. She spoke for the silent Eastman as they came through the gate and along the walk.

"You took your time out there."

Chuck and Wes came up the steps and onto the porch. Rosalie sensed something was wrong.

"Chuck?"

Mona came from inside, closed the door behind her, and stood beside Eastman, who stayed on the bench, crutches at hand.

Mona glared at Wes, hating the sight of him. And with her son.

Chuck looked at all of them, started his report. "Pa, we got a little far north."

Rosalie, Mona, and Eastman watched Chuck's new attitude. Chuck appeared cocky, something that made Rosalie smile.

Chuck took his time, then continued. "Kid Lightning and Miller, and ole Potluck, came riding up. They had their pistols out and aiming right at us."

Chuck still held his hat in front of the weapons in his belt.

Ray Eastman tensed. He looked from Chuck to Wes, who remained silent as Chuck continued, but Ray knew something bad had happened.

"We had to defend ourselves," Chuck said. He moved his hat aside to show the pistols. "So we did."

Rosalie, Eastman, and Mona stared at the three revolvers in Chuck's belt.

Eastman found his voice. "You killed 'em?"

Chuck grinned. "Wes, he was real fast. He got Kid Lightning and Miller, I mean they didn't figure he'd take a chance when they had their pistols on us. Me, I wounded Potluck." He removed pistols from his belt and set them on the porch floor. "We sent Potluck home with the bodies."

They all stared at him. It took time to digest that information.

Chuck tried to look and sound brave. "Pa, they didn't give us no choice. They was gonna kill us or drag us."

Eastman looked at Wes, who nodded agreement.

Mona recovered. "Chuck, I'll have no more of this."

Chuck ignored her. "We got a fight on our hands, right, Pa?"

Eastman stared with pleasure at Chuck, nodded.

"I'm hungry," Chuck said to his mother. "Got anything to eat?"

Mona glared at Chuck, who grinned and walked into the house, Rosalie at his heels. They closed the door behind them.

Mona looked explosive as she turned to Eastman.

"Do something. Don't you see what's happened?"

Eastman nodded. "Our son just became a man."

Mona paused to give Wes a murderous, chilling look. She

turned and stormed into the house. She slammed the door behind her.

Eastman looked at Wes, who leaned on the railing.

"Thanks, Wes."

"What do you think will happen now?" Wes asked.

"Was a time when I'd say nothing, on account of Art Rodecker's been after Rosalie. But she just told me she won't marry him. She's only been seeing him to please Mona and make life easier for me." Eastman gestured toward the north.

"So I figure, we'd better be ready. I'll have Jones alert the men to watch their backs."

Wes straightened. "I'll tell 'im."

"You do that."

Wes turned and walked off the porch.

As he approached the smithy, he could hear Jones hammering away. Wes almost smiled. His father, not even knowing who he was, had just trusted him to alert the men.

Maybe it was a small thing, but not to Wes.

Later that day at the Rodecker ranch, Pete Rodecker climbed onto the corral fence with his son Art. They watched two men working a colt. It was a sunny, warm afternoon.

Pete looked around at the surrounding hillsides, at his cattle, at his own little world where he was king. He frowned at the storm in the Razorbacks holding off when the mesa was so dry.

Art pointed to the distant trail. They all turned to watch Potluck approach with the dead trailing on their horses.

Pete made a face. "What the devil?"

"Looks like they ran into Wes Montana."

"I wasn't ready for this," Pete said.

"That makes four," Art said.

They hopped off the fence. The other men came out of the corral and hurried to meet Potluck. They brought him and the dead up to the corral. The two hands helped Potluck down.

Potluck, bleeding and dazed, swayed on his feet. They helped him over to sit on the edge of the watering trough. Potluck wheezed. "Wes Montana and that kid, Chuck, they throwed down on us."

Potluck slid off the watering trough, onto the ground. He sat bleeding against it. His voice was hoarse. His eyes were vacant, but he kept on with his report.

"Montana got Lightning and Miller. The damn Eastman kid got me." He gasped in pain. "Never knew he had any guts."

Pete paused, studied him. "Who drew first?"

"We had our guns out when we came on 'em."

"This Montana, he's that fast?"

"Didn't even see his hand move."

"And Chuck Eastman?"

"Caught me off guard."

The two cowhands lifted Potluck to his feet. Potluck cursed under his breath, swayed, closed his eyes, and was gone.

The men lowered him back to the ground. Potluck rolled out flat. Nobody was grieving.

Art and Pete started walking toward the house. "No waiting now," Pete said.

Art hesitated. "So what are you going to do?"

"We got forty hands to their twenty or so."

"They ride for the brand," Art said, "but they ain't gun hands."

"We got six professionals."

"You're right, as long as they're paid."

"They only have Montana," Pete said.

Art and Pete reached the porch of the house. Pete turned to his son.

"But first, you gotta get Rosalie to say yes."

"I'm supposed to picnic with her tomorrow. I'll ask again,

but she'll say no."

"What makes you so sure?"

Art shrugged. "The way she acts."

"That's how women are."

"Maybe Eastman won't let her off his ranch, what with so many dead now."

"Mona will make sure she comes."

"All right."

"Whatever Rosalie says, bring her here. And don't let her leave."

"What do you have in mind?"

"It's time to bring this to a head."

Late that night, with Chuck upstairs and Mona asleep in a back bedroom on the first floor, Rosalie was alone with Ray Eastman in the parlor. She stood in her robe by the warm fire in the hearth. She looked contented.

He sat in a stuffed chair, fully dressed, his bad leg propped up with his boot on a stool. He looked mean.

Rosalie turned with a smile. "Ray, I think you just never want to turn in. Maybe you think if you stay dressed, you'll live forever."

"Don't sass me, young lady."

"I thought it reminded you of my grandfather."

"Old Bob, yeah, he had a sharp Irish tongue, all right."

"So . . ."

"So you're not Bob. You're a little girl who's supposed to be a lady."

"Describe lady."

"Just pay attention. And stay away from Montana."

"But he's delicious."

"A cold-blooded killer."

"No one's accused him of murder."

"No," Eastman said, "but he's too fast and too deadly for a fair fight. And don't try to change the subject. Stay away from him."

"Maybe he just needs someone to love."

"What? What kind of talk is that for a little girl?"

"I'm twenty."

"Well, he's too old for the likes of you."

"He looks older, I know, but he's only twenty-four."

"How do you know that?"

"They thought I was asleep in the cabin."

"That's one of your tricks, all right."

She came over to sit on the arm of his chair. She tousled his thinning hair. He tried to look mean, but her sweetness always won him over. He tried to fight it.

"I wish your grandfather could see you now," Eastman grunted. "He thought you'd turn out sweet and gentle."

"Ray, I am sweet and gentle."

"That's a laugh."

She smiled, smoothed his hair. "I'm everything you want me to be, at the moment."

"Then stay away from Montana."

"I like him."

"He didn't get fast with a gun by being nice to folks."

"But I know you like him."

Eastman shrugged. "From a man's point of view, but you ain't no man."

She tickled his hair, then smoothed it.

"Did you know he plays a harmonica? So sweet, it makes you want to cry. A window to his soul."

"He's got no soul."

"It's the only way he can talk to you."

Eastman was half-asleep with her hand soft on his brow. She spoke softly.

"He plays 'Red River Valley' most of the time." Shook her head. "It was his mother's favorite. And after what happened to her, he has a right to be bitter."

There was a brief silence. Eastman started to listen, pay attention.

"What are you talking about?"

"I heard him tell Jedidiah. His mother was murdered. About three months ago."

Ray Eastman was tense. "What else?"

"Not much. Jedidiah said she was a real lady though." She thought a moment, remembered. "Oh, and she's buried at the Claymore ranch."

"What?"

Eastman was explosive; he sat up so fast it caused her to jump up from her seat on the chair arm. Rosalie was a little frightened, just for a moment.

Eastman demanded, "What was her name?"

"I don't know."

"Who was his father?"

"I don't know."

Eastman tried to grab his crutches. They fell to the floor.

"I'm going out and talk with him."

"He'll be asleep. And you'll fall down in the dark."

"Give me those crutches."

She handed him his crutches. He got up awkwardly.

"I'd better go with you."

"You'll do no such thing." He turned, shouted. "Chuck!"

The whole house rattled with his voice. The fire flickered.

Rosalie was taken aback, her mouth open.

"Chuck!" Eastman roared again.

Chuck ran down the stairs, wearing no shirt over his long red underwear and britches. He still wore his gun belt, boots, and hat. His six-gun was in his hand.

"What? Where? What happened?"

"I want you to take me outside."

"What?"

"Come on, it's moonlight enough."

Chuck, half-asleep, obliged. He helped his father outside.

Mona came out of the back bedroom, drawing her robe about her as the cold night forced Rosalie to close the front door.

"What's going on?"

"Oh, a bad dream maybe," Rosalie said. "Chuck went for a walk with his father."

"Ray is getting too old," Mona said.

"Chuck will take care of him."

Mona turned and went back to the bedroom.

Rosalie tried to peer through the curtains, but it was too dark outside. She couldn't understand Eastman's rantings.

Outside in the moonlight, Chuck, half-dressed, six-gun in hand, walked with his hobbling father over toward the smithy. The night was moon bright but dreary.

"It's too cold out here, Pa."

"Keep moving."

Chuck kept yawning. His father growled, nearly fell. They neared the back shed by the smithy. Music drifted from the structure. Harmonica, fiddle, and guitar. Lamps glowed inside.

Eastman paused to listen. The harmonica was soft and sweet, playing the strains of "Red River Valley."

Chuck grinned. "That's Jones on his old beat-up guitar. And Shorty with his fiddle."

"And the mouth organ?"

"Oh, that's Montana."

Eastman listened a moment longer. Then he bellowed like thunder.

"Wes Montana! You get out here."

Horses jumped in the corral. Everything shook. Music stopped.

Chuck winced. "You just busted my ears."

"Montana!"

"What you want with him, Pa?"

"He's been lying to me."

"Take it easy, Pa. Wes is okay. I like him."

"Montana!"

"Don't scare him off, Pa."

Jones and Shorty hurried out of the shed with their instruments, darted around Eastman and Chuck, and headed for the bunkhouse as fast as they could walk. They disappeared inside.

Chuck kept his father standing, facing the smithy shed.

There was a long wait. Horses ran around in the corrals.

No sign of Wes.

"I'm going in," Eastman said.

Chuck helped him into the open entrance where lamplight made a soft glow in the shed.

Wes, sitting on a barrel, pocketed his harmonica and stood.

Eastman managed to sit on a large wooden crate.

Wes was fully dressed.

Eastman cleared his throat. "Chuck, you go on back. Montana can walk me to the house."

"But, Pa—"

"I said, go."

"Yeah, sure, now I'm wide awake."

"Don't give me no sass. Go on back."

Chuck hesitated. Eastman growled.

"Go!"

Chuck jumped, looked at the silent Wes, then at his father. He shrugged, grinned at Wes as if to say he was on his own, turned, and walked toward the house.

Chuck paused again, looked back, then continued back to

the house and up the steps, inside and out of sight.

Behind the smithy in the lamplight, Eastman was alone with Wes and seated. Eastman gestured.

"Sit down, Montana."

Wes sat down warily. The lamplight cast a glow on Eastman's grim face.

So many things Eastman wanted to know but was afraid to ask, so he started with Wes's first visit.

"You claim I got a letter from Mary."

Wes nodded, didn't answer.

"Never saw it, but Mona could have torn it up," Eastman said. "Be like her."

Wes picked up a stick, scratched the dirt.

Eastman took a deep breath. He was terrified of what he was about to learn, so afraid he did not try to understand.

Eastman choked on his words. "So my Mary didn't die in the blizzard?"

Wes shook his head.

"How is it possible?"

"She survived in a snow cave. Jedidiah found her. Took her to Claymore's. They're old friends. When Jedidiah heard about you being alive, he wrote Claymore. And that's when she sent you a letter, right after."

"So Claymore's not dead?"

Wes shook his head, looked away.

"I can't believe she was alive all these years."

Wes didn't respond.

Eastman had to know about her life without him. "And she never married anyone else?"

Wes shook his head. Eastman felt sadness and relief.

"She lived at the Claymores'?"

"She worked for him, helped his wife."

Eastman took a deep breath. "And there was no other man in her life?"

Wes shook his head. Eastman waited for Wes to say something, anything.

Wes was too pressured to answer. He remained silent. Eastman was getting exasperated.

"How can I believe any of this?"

It was time, but Wes was hesitant for a long moment. Then he reached inside his vest, took out the amulet.

Slowly, Wes stood and walked to Eastman. He held the amulet out, placing it on Eastman's palm.

"My God," Eastman whispered. He fondled the amulet, clutched it in his hand.

Wes returned to his seat.

Eastman tried to stand, sat back down. Holding the amulet turned back the years like a thunderstorm, leaving him even more shaken.

Eastman wiped at his eyes with the back of his hand. Then he stared at this dangerous, deadly gunfighter who had come out of nowhere.

They gazed at each other like men who had just walked from a dark night into blazing sun. Blinded, dazed.

Eastman was an emotional and physical wreck. It was still hard for him to digest.

It was even harder for Wes, who wasn't sure he wanted Eastman to know he was his son. Rejection would be too painful. And how could he then kill the man?

Eastman began once more to pursue the truth. "So she really did send a letter?"

Wes nodded, dug at the dirt. "Right after, she was murdered. One of the hands had been on guard when she was out at the creek. They slit his throat."

Eastman seemed to feel her pain. "And they never figured

who done it?"

"Tracks of three men and horses, that's all."

Long pause as Eastman swallowed the information. "And you thought I sent 'em?" Eastman asked.

Wes slowly looked up. His dark eyes were gleaming. Wes nodded as Eastman stared at him.

It was hard to say, but Wes nodded, managed to get it out. "I came here to kill you."

Eastman was rattled. "And now?"

It took a moment for Wes to accept his father's likely innocence. All the hate, the fury, still buried in Wes, was trying to dissipate.

But Wes looked at his father's dismay and knew the truth. "I was wrong."

Eastman held his breath, waiting for more, and it came as Wes looked directly at him and spoke softly.

"Mary was my mother."

Wes's admission stunned Eastman. He was hurting, afraid to think Mary, the love of his life, had been with another man. It took him a moment to ask a painful question, not really wanting to know.

"But who was your father?"

Eastman was tied in knots as Wes spoke more softly. "When Jedidiah found her in a snow cave, she was barely alive. He nursed her back to life."

Ray Eastman was waiting, his breath burning.

Wes swallowed hard and continued. "I was born seven months later."

There was a long silence as Eastman accepted what he was hearing as the truth. He stared at Wes in amazement.

"You're her son? My son?"

Wes nodded. He, too, felt the shock of the moment.

"My God. But this being a hired gun, why . . ."

"I got respect."

"And no one dared call you a breed."

Wes shook his head, glad Eastman understood.

"The name Montana?"

"They made it up. They thought you were dead and your kin might come to take me away."

"I had no kin."

Wes and his father gazed at each other a long moment in the flickering lamplight. Joy was flooding Eastman.

"I want the whole darn world to know you're my son. My firstborn."

Wes felt the pleasure of Eastman's words, but he shook his head. "Better to wait. Find out who killed her."

"You're right. We'll hold off, smoke 'em out."

Wes and Eastman were silent a moment. Then Eastman spoke.

"But I'm writing an instruction to my lawyer. You'll have equal shares with Chuck and Rosalie. Both of 'em, they'll protect your right as my son. And no one will dare call you a half-breed." Deep breath. "And Mona will take her share in money and leave you be."

Wes didn't know how to react, what to feel. All the hate Wes had harbored had no place to go.

"Tonight, I had about decided to ride off," Wes said, "and never look back."

"Without either one of us knowing the truth?"

"I couldn't bring myself to—"

"Kill me?"

"You had a wife and son."

"Wes, I have two sons."

Eastman wiped his mouth, struggled with his words.

"You'll get what's due, Wes." He grinned. "And now you have a half brother."

"He's a good kid. He's full of it, but he's a heck of a shot."

Eastman grinned, then sobered. He studied Wes, liking him so much it hurt. He was so overwhelmed by what he had learned tonight, he figured he'd never sleep again.

They sat staring at each other.

"I'm sorry I wasn't there to be a father, to raise you up. I know how it feels, because I was left on the steps at an orphanage before I could walk. They had to give me a name. I got to be such a bad kid, no one wanted me, so I finally ran away at fourteen. That's when I met Bob Riley. He took me trapping, made a man out of me. The mountains was where I found Mary. But I've always wondered where I came from, and I'll never know. So I'm glad you have it all found out."

Wes felt a deep connection with his father, a man who knew what it was like to be alone. Eastman took up his crutches. "I'd better get back. But you won't leave me, Wes."

"No, sir."

Eastman was so filled with pleasure it hurt. "Now help me back to the house, will you?"

Wes walked along with Eastman, who hobbled with more strength and spirit. Eastman had his arm around Wes's shoulder for stability, but his grip was tight, relishing his newfound son.

At the porch, Eastman turned to look at Wes. "Promise me you'll stay."

"You have my word."

They shook hands strongly. Eastman hesitated, his voice broken.

"Goodnight . . . Son."

It was even harder for Wes to respond.

"Goodnight . . . Pa."

Their connection was so deep, it hurt.

Ray Eastman turned and hobbled up the steps without help. On the porch, Eastman turned to look back at Wes, who stood looking up at him with a softer gaze and deeper understanding.

Eastman grinned. "God Almighty!" Wes managed a half smile back but sobered when the door opened.

Lamplight from inside spread over Eastman on the porch and Wes at the foot of the steps.

Wes saw Rosalie and Chuck in the doorway. Wes tipped his hat, turned and walked away. He went back inside the shed and sat down, exhausted, traumatized. He bowed his head to whisper a prayer.

Rosalie waited as Chuck helped Eastman inside and closed the door behind them.

Eastman's eyes were wet, but he smiled with his secret. Chuck and Rosalie were not used to seeing him smile.

Rosalie was worried. "Ray?"

Eastman began to grin from ear to ear. "Son of a gun!"

He pulled away and hobbled down the hallway on his crutches. They stared after him.

They saw Mona greet him in the hallway and fuss over him. Eastman did not yell at her.

Back in the parlor, Chuck pushed his hat back. "What the heck is he so happy about?"

Rosalie smiled. "Whatever it is, I love it." A happy Rosalie turned to go up the stairs.

Chuck, scratching his head, turned to follow.

In the bedroom, Mona helped Eastman sit on the bed. She pulled off his boots, one at a time. He was grinning in the lamplight.

She was worried. "Ray, are you all right?"

"Sure am."

"What were you doing out there?"

"Baying at the moon." He laid down, grinning, still fully clothed.

Mona was more than worried.

★ ★ ★ ★ ★

The next morning at the Eastman ranch, Rosalie stood on the porch with a picnic basket. She wore her nicest outfit, a navy skirt and pale blue jacket over a white blouse. She even wore a woman's broad-brimmed hat instead of a man's.

Mona, smiling, moved to her side.

"Mona, I don't want to do this."

"Someday you'll be glad you did."

"I'm not going to marry Art."

"Don't sass me. He asks you again, you'll say yes. Or I'll send you away."

"Ray won't let you."

Mona drew herself up, shivered, then sniffed.

"Rosalie, I've tried to be a mother to you because you lost your family. I still remember you as a skinny girl in dirty clothes, carrying that squeaky old music box."

Rosalie had learned how Mona liked to manipulate. She remained silent as the woman continued.

"You'll do this for me, if you love me. If I was free, I'd do it myself, just to keep peace on the mesa."

"You'd marry Art?"

"Don't talk to me that way." Mona softened. "I don't have an easy life, you know that. Ray is so difficult and so uncivilized." Mona paused for effect, then continued. "I need you to do this for me. Please try."

Rosalie nodded despite herself.

Chuck came wandering outside. He wore no shirt, exposing his red underwear, which he scratched. He wore his hat, britches, and boots. And his sidearm.

Jones led Rosalie's mare over to the porch. It had her sidesaddle. Jones took her picnic basket and tied it to the back of the saddle over a blanket.

Chuck scratched again. "Where you going, Rosalie?"

Rosalie was too upset to answer.

Mona glared at Chuck. "She's going to picnic with Art. She's meeting him halfway. Somehow, we have to stop all this killing."

"Pa won't like it."

Mona stiffened. "You and that . . . that Wes Montana, you nearly started a war. And stop that scratching."

"Something bit me in that fancy bed. Some bug just out of finishing school."

Rosalie giggled, tried to get sober again.

Mona glared at Chuck. "So this is how you are now? You think it's so wonderful to shoot a helpless man?"

"Helpless? Ma, they were going to drag and kill us."

"Just talk."

"I'm glad it happened," Chuck said. "Pa likes me better."

"That's not a good reason," Mona snapped.

"Good enough for me."

Chapter Eight

Later that day on the north mesa, Rosalie and Art were settled by a little creek, sheltered by trees, and had finished eating.

They both glanced often at the black clouds still hovering over the far-off Razorbacks.

They sat on a blanket, enjoying the scenery. But now the wind was rising. Rosalie folded the picnic cloth and put it in the basket of empty dishes.

Art helped her to her feet. He was always a gentleman. She tried to appreciate him.

The wind struck with sudden force, tearing at her clothes and hat, which she held in place.

"Art, the wind is terrible. We'd better hurry."

"Hope it brings rain. The river's about hit bottom."

She nodded, fighting to hold her hat.

Art put on his niceness. "I'm sorry I've been pushing you to marry me, but I can't help myself." He hesitated, lied. "All I knew growing up was Pa, and he can be a tyrant. That's why I need someone sweet like you."

Rosalie smiled. "No one would say I'm sweet."

She helped him fold the blanket. Liked him more than she expected. But he was no Wes Montana. He carried the blanket as they walked to the horses.

She took the basket. Despite her hat, her hair blew wild in the wind.

She glanced at him with a smile. "I thought you were like

your father. You're not so bad after all."

Art tied the blanket and basket to the back of her saddle. "Glad to hear that." He turned, took her hand. "I'd like it if you were to come to the ranch with me. You've never been there. And there's still time to get you back home."

"That wouldn't be seemly."

"We have a woman who keeps house for us, a Mexican lady. She's a widow, lost her man to a bronc. You'll like her." He paused, then added, "And Mrs. Eastman told me it would be all right."

Rosalie hesitated, but she had never seen their ranch and was curious.

At the Rodecker ranch in midafternoon, Rosalie allowed Art to help her dismount. The sun was warm, but the wind was harsh. A storm could come fast, which worried her.

Art was overly attentive. Despite herself, she liked him. They walked up the steps to the porch and opened the door into the house.

"Anna will take care of you," he said. "I'll join you in a few minutes."

Inside, she was greeted by Anna, who wore a red shawl over her apron and plain clothes. She looked very pretty.

The room was plush, with a tiny fire in the grand hearth, but Rosalie was more interested in Anna, who spoke better American than most. Anna was apparently well-educated and likely from a family of aristocrats. Anna was very friendly and made her feel comfortable.

But Anna's eyes were wet. Rosalie spoke softly to her. "Are you in trouble?"

Anna responded to Rosalie's kindness.

"My husband and I were both working here, but he died last year, when a horse fell on him. His family took our children until I could save money. They lived just south of Salt Lake City, but they moved away and left my boys in a children's home. I can't get them unless I pay for all the room and board they've had." She dabbed at her eyes. "And now that home wants some of the payment now or they'll sell them."

"How can they do that?"

"People will pay to adopt them."

"Do you have family?"

"In Mexico, but they disowned me when I married."

"Maybe we can help you." Anna perked up, hopeful. "If I can get out of here," Rosalie said.

Anna hesitated. "They are bad men here."

"I know."

Art came into the house. "Anna, bring some tea."

Anna nodded and went down the hall, then out of sight. His glance followed her.

"Anna's a tough lady," Art said. "She won't have nothing to do with Pa." Grinned. "Just as well."

"Because she's Mexican?"

"Because Anna's hard as nails. She'd cut him up with her carving knife before he could get near her."

Rosalie smiled. "Good for her."

Rosalie took time to look around and enjoy the luxury of the grand house: the great stone hearth in the parlor, rosewood furniture, fine paintings, dark red rug, crimson drapes. A tall grandfather's clock chimed four o'clock.

"This is grand, Art. We have a few fancy things, but not in a house like this."

Art walked over and took Rosalie's hand. "All you have to do is marry me, and you'll be the queen of all this."

"Please don't rush me, Art."

"I thought we were getting to be friends."

"We are, but Ray would never allow it."

"Mona will win him over." He paused to bend over and kiss her hand. "Promise me you'll think about it?"

She nodded, reluctant.

"We'll have tea before we ride back."

"No, Art, it's getting too late. That wind could bring bad weather."

He ignored her worry, smiled, and led her to the sofa.

Again, Rosalie resisted, but she sat on the sofa with him as Anna brought the tea on a silver tray and set it on the table in front of them. Then Anna left.

Rosalie poured. Art watched her longingly.

She was nervous. "I didn't see any of your men around."

"Most are on the range. Looks like a norther. If we get dry lightning, we could have a stampede. Maybe a grass or brush fire."

"That's why I'd better go home, now."

"My father will want to see you, and he'll be back any minute."

Out on the mesa, a strong, violent wind was still rising from the north.

Thor and Clem Welsh had been drinking. They rode south to the wide river and had a look toward the rolling land of the Eastman spread.

Thor hooked a leg over the horn, rolled a smoke. His bandanna drooped enough to show an ugly rope burn on his neck.

Clem held tight to his hat in the wind. "Never thought we'd see Wes Montana," Clem said. "He scares me plenty. Wish ole Rango was here to back us up."

"Rango could get us hanged."

"He keeps his mouth shut, we'll be okay."

Thor nodded. "Yeah."

"I'd rather be shot full of holes," Clem said, touching his neck. "Hanging's the worst way a man can die."

"Them vigilantes sure tried."

"Yeah, when the boys cut us down, I swore we'd never go through that again. These burns on our necks make sure we don't forget."

Both felt their necks under their bandannas.

"Never again," Thor said. "I still have nightmares."

Clem nodded.

They looked back to see the distant and vast Rodecker herd restless in the high gusts. Some thirty hands were trying to circle them.

"That norther coming in, there's not enough men to stop 'em," Thor said. "Them cattle will be in California afore it's over."

They both looked to the black clouds hovering over the Razorbacks. It might never come down to the mesa. Even then, it could bring lightning but no rain.

Clem huddled with his back to the wind, finished rolling the smoke, and licked to seal it.

Thor pulled a bottle from his saddlebag, took a sip.

"I ain't getting run over by no stampede."

Clem hiccupped. "Remember that time on the trail when a norther carried half the cattle off?"

Clem swayed in the saddle, took out his matches. The rolled tobacco was held by his lips.

Thor grunted. "We was too drunk to know it." He looked around. "What are we doing here, anyhow?"

"Getting paid."

Clem struck a match and lighted his smoke with his back to the roaring wind.

Thor glared at him. "You'd better be careful there. That grass is tinder dry."

Clem puffed on his smoke, smothered the match. "I'll bet you five bucks that there wind will carry this smoke clear across the river."

"You're on."

Clem sent the rolled, burning tobacco into the air. It sailed in the wind, across the shallow river.

The smoke cleared the water, ended up in Eastman's dry grass.

Clem gestured. "Another five, it starts to burn."

They sat their saddles, passing the bottle back and forth.

They waited with the wind tearing at them as they hung on to their hats. Thor drank the bottle dry and tossed it aside.

Clem laughed, pointing to the smoke rising from the far grass on Eastman's side.

Thor tried to shake the alcohol from his senses.

Thor caught himself up. "We'd better get out of here."

"It rains, it'll put it out."

They looked at the darkening sky to the east, then turned and rode back toward the distant herd.

The smoke smoldered in the grass, caught fire. The wind fanned the tiny flames as they rose from the dry grass and burned south.

Thor and Clem never looked back.

Back at the Rodecker ranch, Rosalie walked outside on the porch with Art on her heels. The strong wind was tearing at everything. It blew her hair. She pulled on her hat, tightened the chin strap.

Dark clouds still hovered over the distant Razorbacks.

"I can't wait for your father, Art."

They looked south and saw smoke rising. A black cloud beyond the river. She was horrified.

"It's on fire."

"Calm down. You stay here and if there's a way that's safe, I'll—"

"I'm going with you."

She hurried down to her mare. Reluctant, he went down to give her a foot up.

Before he could mount his own horse, she was already riding at a lope toward the river.

The grass fire was soon out of control along the south side of the river and racing south on the Eastman half of the mesa. Wind blew the smoke toward the Eastman ranch.

Beyond, in the east hills, Eastman's vast herd of cattle and near a hundred horses were crazed as the Eastman riders tried to head them east, away from the fire.

The herd was like a roll of thunder, out of control.

Jones, Wes, and Shorty joined the others. Jones shouted to the nearest hands.

"Head for the ponds."

The hands brought the herd around and headed east toward the ponds near the base of the Razorbacks.

At the ranch house, Ray Eastman was standing on the porch with his crutches, watching the smoke that was filling the sky. The fire was headed south, toward his ranch buildings.

Eastman, Mona, and Chuck were the only ones left on the place, since all the hands had ridden to corral the herd against the rising wind and smoke. The storm still hovered over the Razorbacks.

Mona came onto the porch.

Chuck, down at the corral, had set most of the horses free. He harnessed a team to a wagon and drove it over to the house. His saddle horse was tied behind. There was a barrel of water, food, rolled blankets, slickers, and axes in the wagon bed.

Mona and Eastman stared from Chuck to the smoke.

Mona looked frightened. "What is it?"

"Prairie fire," Eastman said. "We're cut off from the valley trail. We have to get out of here. Over to the ponds."

"My gowns."

"Too late. Get in the wagon." He looked around. "Where's Rosalie?"

"On a picnic with Art Rodecker."

Eastman was furious. "He's saving her to get the ranch legal. While we all burn . . ."

Mona wasn't listening—she was too afraid of the fire.

Eastman turned to glare at the fire. "Looks like they figured to get rid of the lot of us."

Chuck came up on the porch. "The wagon's loaded. I'll get the coats and more blankets." He ran inside the house.

Eastman smiled. "That boy's going to be all right."

Eastman worked his way to the steps, with Mona following. They saw Wes riding toward them at full gallop. Behind Wes, they saw the black smoke rising. Ash was already stinging the air. Wes's buckskin slid to a stop and turned.

"Where's Jones?" Eastman asked.

"Heading the cattle to the ponds. You can still get there."

Chuck came out with coats and blankets, looked around.

Wes held his hat tight in the wind.

Chuck turned to Eastman. "Pa, can you drive the wagon?"

"Yeah, I can brake with my good leg."

"You should be okay on the wagon road. If you hurry."

Chuck handed Eastman and Mona their coats. He went down and put the blankets in the wagon bed. Eastman and Mona donned their coats, and Mona headed down to the wagon.

Chuck helped his father down the steps and up onto the seat. He handed Eastman his crutches and the lines. Mona climbed up beside Eastman. The dog leaped into the back.

"Pa, you both go on. We'll try to save the house."

Mona looked worried. "Chuck, you come with us."

Chuck freed and mounted his horse and rode up alongside the wagon.

"Ma, I'm staying with Wes."

Ray Eastman fought his sudden panic. He wanted Chuck to know the truth, just in case. He didn't want to die without telling him.

"Watch yourself. I can't lose both my sons."

Chuck stared at him. "What?"

Mona grimaced. "Don't listen to your father."

"Wes Montana is my first-born," Eastman told Chuck.

Wes felt his face turn hot, his heart wild.

Chuck looked from Eastman to Wes and back again in dismay.

"She was a dirty old Indian," Mona said. "It doesn't mean anything."

"She was my wife," Eastman said.

Mona snapped. "With some beads and a blanket?"

Chuck, choked up, looking from Wes to Eastman as the smoke rolled closer and closer in the rushing wind. Ashes fell on them and the horses.

Chuck's face began to fill with delight. "Pa, is it true?"

Eastman fingered the reins, nodded to Chuck.

Mona fretted. "He's a breed."

Chuck stared, still incredulous. He looked at Wes, then at his father.

"He's my half brother?"

Eastman nodded. "That's right."

Chuck shook his head. "Lord a-Mighty." He was grinning, unable to contain his joy.

Wes choked with the recognition. The scowl on Mona's face didn't faze him, but Chuck's delight was filling Wes with wonder. Yet there wasn't time to enjoy the revelation.

Wes gestured to Eastman. "Better get moving."

"We will, son," Eastman said to Wes.

Wes had a sober look but his heart was pounding. He turned to Chuck. "Jones said you had dynamite here."

"That old stuff? We buried it, but I can find it. Come on."

Mona was frantic. "Charles!"

Chuck and Wes rode away toward the smithy.

"Ray, Charles will get hurt."

"They're brothers. They'll take care of each other."

"Brothers? That half-breed? How can you shame me like that?"

Ray Eastman set the wagon team off at a trot along the wagon road, south of the smoke, heading east toward the ponds.

Mona glared at his profile, at the smile on his face, even as ashes were falling on them.

On the north mesa, Rosalie, riding ahead of Art Rodecker, was frantic at the sight of the smoke as the wind carried the fire toward the Eastman ranch. The flames and smoke crossed the land in front of her.

She was forced to rein up by the river. Art Rodecker rode up beside her. He reined to a halt.

"I've got to get through," she said.

"You can't ride over burned ground," he said. "Besides, they must have moved out by now. Off the mesa. Or over by the water."

"But the ranch house . . ."

Rosalie was thinking of Ray and Chuck. And Wes. And now of her music box, the only memory of her mother and father, about to be lost.

Art shook his head. "The wind's so bad, I don't think they can even get a backfire going."

"How did it start?"

Art rode along the river where the scorched earth was just smoldering but impassable on the other side. He saw an empty whiskey bottle near the bank, and he reined up.

Rosalie joined him.

"Maybe a careless hand with a smoke." He turned his horse to her side. "Let me take you back to our ranch. There's nothing you can do."

"We could ride on this side of the river, toward the Razorbacks, get over to the ponds."

"Not safe. The wind can change."

He gestured to the black smoke heaving with the wind to the east, even as the storm still hovered over the Razorbacks.

"Maybe it will rain," she said with little hope. Rosalie was worried but resigned. She turned her horse with his.

On the south mesa along the wagon road, Mona and Eastman rode in the rig with the dog in back. Ray urged the team onward. He tried to get around the billowing smoke and over to the ponds near the Razorbacks. Smoke was blinding them now.

Eastman turned the team, whipped them into a trot, then a lope. The wagon careened along the dirt path, hit rocks, bounced.

Mona panicked. "Ray, slow down!"

The rig hit the edge of a creek bed.

"Look out, you fool!"

The horses reared, throwing them both from the rig as the wagon rolled half on its side. The dog leaped into the creek.

Eastman rolled into the creek alongside the road. It was shallow but plenty wet. He was stunned, but not hurt.

Mona fell but clung to the side of the wagon and was only shaken.

Eastman crawled up the bank to the stuck wagon as the team reared and whinnied. The dog stayed with him. Smoke was all around them. Flames were but fifty feet away.

Eastman, soaked, ignored the pain in his leg. He struggled to reach the wagon from the creek side, grabbing the rear wheel. He could not budge it.

Holding onto the wagon, Eastman fought his way, hand over hand to the front of the wagon and the frantic team. He grabbed the halter and harness of the right horse and held on until it stopped rearing. He pulled the team forward to free the wheel.

The fire leaped into the air, red through the smoke, coming at them at a rapid pace.

Their only chance of survival was the wagon. Mona climbed up and on the wagon seat. He handed her the lines. She moved over to put her foot on the brake.

Eastman, in great pain, started to climb up toward the seat.

When the horses began to rear in the smoke, Eastman turned back to calm them and was slammed aside by the horses. He was thrown back down into the creek, badly hurt.

Mona set the brake and held the team. She looked down at Eastman, who lay half in the water and could not move. He needed help, but she didn't seem ready to climb down to him. She released the brake, picked up the lines.

He realized she was about to leave him. "Mona!"

The dog was in the creek with Eastman, licking his face and arm. It gripped his sleeve with its teeth and pulled.

"Mona! For God's sake."

Mona stared down at the helpless Eastman. She looked at the raging firestorm that was almost upon them. Already the smoke was swallowing them, with flames shooting forward just yards away.

Mona wanted him to die. She could have Pete Rodecker. She would be queen of the mesa. She watched as Eastman tried to get up, fell back.

Her eyes were wild. She slapped the lines as the team fought the harness. She took one last look at the helpless Eastman then drove the frantic team away from him, east around the smoke. She disappeared as the smoke closed in behind her.

The deadly smoke was upon Ray and his dog. He started digging the soft bank, making a hollow, scooping the wet dirt up and over him from the waist up. The dog started digging.

With his lower body in the creek, Eastman, along with the dog, was safely covered with mud when the fire swept over them with a roar. Eastman used an elbow to allow air as he held to the amulet and prayed.

Mona circled the southbound fire, then drove the wagon north toward Rodecker's. She could see the distant herd of Eastman cattle moving toward the ponds to the east, but she still had a clear path.

When she reached the river crossing, she was free of smoke. She drove across the shallow river and continued north. She was a happy woman.

At the Eastman ranch, Wes and Chuck dug up the old dynamite, which had been buried near the smithy. They put it carefully into gunny sacks. The fire and smoke were still a few hundred yards away.

Chuck was nervous. "This stuff can explode any second. Do you see how it's sweating? Jones says that's nitro."

"Let's go."

"Where?"

Wes gestured. "We're going to blow up the fire."

Chuck whistled softly. "Swell."

"We'll start at that creek."

"Great. I always wanted a big swimming hole."

"We'll spread 'em out. Then ride for it."

They hurried to their horses, hooking the sacks over their

horns. Chuck turned to Wes. His heart was in his face.

"I'm glad you're my brother."

The words hit Wes deep and wonderful. Wes nodded.

"Even though you're scary as all get-out," Chuck said with a laugh. Wes almost smiled.

They turned to mount their horses and rode toward the heavy smoke already approaching the little creek. Flames were licking the grass so close the heat burned their faces.

At the creek, Wes dismounted to lay the short fused sticks along the bank. Chuck rode east along the creek, stopping to dismount every thirty feet to lay a stick of dynamite.

Then they got together, mounted, and rode at a gallop back toward the ranch. As they neared the corrals, the fire hit the dynamite.

The explosions shook the mesa. Leveled the corrals. Blew shingles from the barn.

Chuck and Wes were nearly thrown from the saddle. Their horses faltered, then recovered. Every blast thereafter was an attack on the fire line.

On the north side of the mesa, north of the fire, Rosalie and Art put distance between them and the smoke. Grass and brush smoldered on the south side.

They heard the explosions, again and again, to the south. They saw smoke billowing to the sky.

"What is it?" she asked.

"I don't know."

They retreated further north and soon dismounted to rest their horses. Rosalie was traumatized.

"My God."

Art put his arm around her as she trembled.

"Don't worry, I'll take care of you."

She leaned her head on his shoulder, grateful for comfort.

CHAPTER NINE

On the east mesa, the explosions could be heard as Jones, Shorty, and the Eastman riders circled the vast herd near the ponds. Jones wiped at his eyes as he heard another explosion. He believed everyone was dead.

"God Almighty," Jones said.

Jones paused to look in the direction of the ranch house, which was already hidden from view by smoke. The way was blocked. No flames were visible. Travers rode over to him.

Jones grimaced. "Tell the boys to keep the cattle near the water. If the fire turns this way, get 'em wet. But it looks to be burning itself out." He held on to his hat. "If that norther hits, we'll have our hands full."

On the south mesa, at the ranch, Chuck and Wes reined about near the smithy. They looked at the storm still hovering over the Razorbacks, then again at the dwindling smoke.

The main thrust of the fire had been broken by the dynamite. The wind was still blowing ash and smoke, but no flames were visible.

"Wes, you saved the ranch."

"You mean, we did."

They rode over to the watering trough and dismounted. They scooped debris from the water. They washed their faces, then let the horses drink.

Chuck pumped fresh water with the hand pump. They drank

from the scoop. They led their horses to the bunkhouse, loosened the cinches, and let them breathe. They sat down on the bench in front of the bunkhouse, exhausted.

Chuck turned to Wes. "Tell me about your ma."

Wes was willing and told his grim story.

After a time, Chuck thought deeply about Wes's story. Wes got to his feet. Chuck scrambled to stand.

Chuck gestured. "That letter. Yeah. From Arizona Territory? Ma took it, and she tore it up. I was scared to tell Pa."

"Right after, my mother was killed by three men. I thought he sent 'em. But now I know different, because he didn't know. He never saw the letter."

"You're saying . . ."

They both fell silent.

Later in the day, at the east mesa by the ponds, Chuck and Wes joined the circled herd near the water. They drank coffee at the chuck wagon while their horses breathed.

The storm appeared ready to leave the Razorbacks; some darkness was coming to the mesa. Rain would be a blessing.

Jones rode up to them. Travers and Shorty followed. Chuck twisted in the saddle and looked around.

"Where's Pa?" Chuck asked. "And my mother?"

"Ain't seen 'em," Jones said.

"They were headed this way in the wagon."

"Maybe they got cut off."

Chuck's chest rose. "You might want to know, Wes is my half brother."

Jones and Shorty, startled, looked from one to the other.

"Well, you sure ain't much alike," Jones said.

Shorty nodded. "I ain't surprised. There was always something there."

Wes was warmed by his words. Shorty was right.

Chuck gestured north. "We got to get Rosalie away from Rodecker. He's keeping her there."

Jones grimaced. "They'll be expecting you."

"It'll be a trap," Shorty warned.

"We got no choice," Chuck replied.

"You go on," Jones said. "I'll look for your folks."

"Pa was driving," Chuck said, worried.

"Wes, you want some of the men to go with you?" Jones asked.

Wes shook his head. "The two of us can get in a lot easier without being seen. Be dark afore we get there."

"They'll be waiting," Jones said.

"That storm hits," Wes replied, "they'll need more of their men to hold their herd. Won't leave many at the ranch."

"We got our hands just as full," Jones said.

"Don't get hurt," Chuck told him, as he and Wes remounted.

But Travers, who had been listening, rode closer. "I'm going with you."

Wes liked the old-timer; he nodded.

Wes and Chuck turned and set their horses to circle the scorched earth. Travers followed.

Riding west from the ponds along the wagon road toward the ranch, Jones picked up the tracks along the creek. He saw where the wagon cut north around the fire.

It didn't make sense that the wagon did not head for the ponds. He saw where the wheels had been in a rut. He reined up to wipe his face with his bandanna.

He heard scratching, and rode to the edge of the creek. Down the bank, he saw the dog, digging in the mud, not far from the wagon tracks. Jones scrambled down to join the dog and dig. He saw Ray Eastman's coat and hat, and yanked them up.

Eastman, one hand still clinging to the amulet strung around his neck, looked up at Jones, rubbed his eyes, and blinked. He was muddy and wet. He coughed.

"Where's Mrs. Eastman?" Jones asked.

"I don't know."

The dog licked Eastman's face and nose and mouth and eyes. Eastman pushed him away and sat up. He cupped his hands in the creek water to wash his face.

"Stop your drooling," Eastman said to the dog.

Jones, ecstatic, got up to go to his saddle for a canteen. He came back down, sat on his heels. He uncapped the canteen and handed it to Eastman.

Eastman poured some over his eyes, then drank, spat dust from his mouth, and drank some more.

Jones grinned. "I knew you was too ornery to die."

Eastman gripped the amulet dangling from his neck.

On the north mesa it was near twilight and the wind persisted. Wes and Chuck rode toward Rodecker's, circling north of the river, their horses picking their way. Travers trailed as if he were rear guard.

The storm was closing in, dark and gloomy. They could see lightning strikes in the mountains and slopes.

"Going to hit hard," Chuck said.

"Make it easier for us."

"But ripe for stampedes."

"Rodeckers have the same problem."

Chuck nodded. "That'll cut the odds."

Chuck worried over his parents but kept looking at Wes, who nodded in return. The half brothers had made a connection. They both had found a new life.

On the north mesa, Rosalie and Art dismounted some distance north of the river. They looked south toward the dwindling smoke beyond the big creek. Then north to the storm moving onto the mesa.

"I've got to go now," she said.

"No, the wind could change. You could be trapped," Art said. "And that storm's coming in pretty fast. We'll go to my ranch until it's safe."

"I'm leaving."

"I can't let you, Rosalie."

She turned to her horse. "Just give me a step up."

"All right, but you're going back with me."

"No, I'm not."

"Tell them."

She turned to follow his gaze as Pete Rodecker and the Welsh brothers rode toward them. Rosalie and Art stepped back as the three men reined up in front them. The Welsh brothers looked Rosalie over.

Pete gestured. "We could see from the rise. The fire's out. The Eastman ranch is in the clear."

"Better luck next time," Thor said.

Rosalie glared up at Pete. "You set that fire?"

Pete shook his head. "And burn up good grass? That would have been a foolish move." He adjusted his hat. "There are better ways to get Eastman's spread. You're one of 'em."

Rosalie turned to Art. "I don't understand."

Pete grinned at her. "So you don't know you're getting a share of that spread?"

Rosalie shook her head and frowned. "I didn't know. But even if I am, you're not getting it from me."

Pete tugged at his hat brim. "Calm down, honey."

"I will not!"

"Rosalie," Art said. "Your house didn't burn. Your folks are all right."

"I'm leaving."

"You ain't going nowhere," Pete said. "If you don't marry Art, Ray Eastman will be shot dead, and so will Chuck. And that fast gun."

Rosalie looked up at Pete, realizing he meant every word.

She saw the greed in Pete's eyes, the need he had to own the entire mesa, to wipe out the competition.

Rosalie started to mount, but she needed help to get up to her sidesaddle. Art assisted her and then mounted his horse, reined next to her.

The sky was black, rushing. At that moment, they paused. Coming into view, driving the wagon toward them from the east, was Mona. She was ignoring the sudden drizzle. To the north and across the mesa, lightning danced.

Mona pulled up the wagon close to them.

"See, Rosalie?" Art asked. "Nobody was hurt."

Pete Rodecker smiled as Mona halted the team.

Rosalie rode over. "Mona, is everyone all right?"

"I'm so sorry, Rosalie. Ray is dead. He was driving too fast and hit some rocks. He was thrown from the wagon."

Rosalie got tearful.

"What about Chuck? And Wes?"

"They stayed at the ranch, so I don't know."

Rosalie took a deep breath, but she guessed Wes and Chuck would take care of each other.

"Jones and Shorty?" Rosalie asked.

Mona shrugged. "I don't know."

Pete looked at the dark clouds moving over them. There were more lightning flashes.

Pete gestured. "That storm spells stampede. Right off the cliffs. Art, better get more men out to the herd."

"Already there."

Mona met Pete's gaze. Her eyes twinkled, something Rosalie did not miss.

Pete looked content. "Come on then, we have to get you women back to our place."

Rosalie resisted. "I want to go to the ponds."

"You're going with us," Pete said.

"Just do as he says," Mona urged.

"They want to cause trouble," Rosalie said.

"No, dear, they just want us safe."

"They're using us as bait."

At that moment, more lightning flashed, dancing in the dark sky. Heavy rain fell on them. And now there was hail with the rain.

Hail that was heavy and dangerous, pounding them.

It was night and raining when Rosalie, Art, and the two Welsh brothers rode up in front of the house. Pete drove the wagon, Mona at his side, his saddle horse tethered behind, and drew up near them.

The men had given their slickers to the women. But everyone was wet from the pounding hail and rain.

Art dismounted, pulled the struggling Rosalie from her horse, and shoved her up the porch steps.

Pete helped Mona down from the wagon. She stared after Rosalie and Art.

"Ray told Chuck that Wes Montana's his son." Mona watched Art force Rosalie into the house.

"Don't matter," Pete said. "Montana won't be around much longer."

Mona turned and smiled up at Pete, who stayed sober. She took his arm as he turned toward the house.

"I'm a widow now."

Pete nodded with a smile. They moved up onto the porch.

She was excited. "The ranch belongs to me."

"But we still need Rosalie."

"Why?"

"We're holding her until Montana shows up."

"There could be a fight."

"That's what I'm counting on."

"But Chuck—"

"He'll be all right. I promise."

"I love you, Peter."

"I'll have your things brought inside."

Before he opened the door for her, he spoke softly. "Meet you out here on the porch in an hour."

She nodded, ecstatic.

When she was inside the house, Pete closed the door behind her. Rain was heavy. The wind was wild. Pete waited on the porch as the Welsh brothers rode up.

"You got your orders."

"Maybe they won't come," Thor said.

"We've got Rosalie. They'll come."

"We ain't got enough men," Clem said.

"You're professionals. Get it done."

The Welsh brothers turned their horses away in the storm, rode to the corrals.

Later, inside the Rodecker ranch house, Mona's carpet bag was left near the stairs. Rain was loud on the roof and at the windows.

Mona was in the parlor with Art and Rosalie. They were seated in chairs and having coffee by the hearth. Anna filled a cup for Mona, who gave her no recognition.

Anna sensed the slight, but Rosalie smiled at her.

Rosalie was wrapped in a blanket. She had been crying.

Anna left the room.

Mona managed to look tearful.

"I'm sorry about Ray," Mona said.

Rosalie hid her face, wiped at her tears.

"But we have a new life now," Mona added.

Art lifted his cup. "To a new life." Rosalie looked up and glared at them. Mona turned it on for Rosalie.

"Rosalie, are you all right?"

"No, Mona, I'm not. We're both prisoners here. They are using us to lay a trap, to kill everyone they can and take over the mesa."

"Rosalie, you're so dramatic," Mona said. "You can't really believe all that."

"Mona's right," Art said. "We're just keeping you safe."

Mona wiped her eyes of false tears, and sipped her coffee.

Rosalie was grim. "But you know they'll be after us. And if you don't let us go, there will be a fight."

"Maybe so," Art said.

"Rosalie, don't make such a fuss." Mona looked sad. "Poor Ray. He loved this mesa so much. But he left the ranch to me, and I don't know anything about running it. I'm afraid I'll have to sell. But it will allow you to travel. Meet new friends."

Rosalie fell silent, realizing Mona didn't know about the change in the will, but Rosalie wasn't sure if it was true.

Art and Mona exchanged glances.

Mona set aside her cup. "I'm very tired." She stood up. "Where can I freshen up?"

Art gestured. "You can use that room down the hall on the right, last one. A bit small, but . . ."

Mona stiffened. "That might be all right for Rosalie."

Art smiled. "Okay, upstairs, first door on the right is the guest room."

Mona paused, waiting to see if Rosalie would go with her. Rosalie just stared into the fire. Mona shrugged, walked over to get her carpet bag, and climbed the stairs.

Art watched her until she was on the landing and had entered the guest room.

Rain and hail continued to pound the roof. Wind rattled the walls. Art took Rosalie's cup to the hearth, filled it from the dangling pot, and returned it to her.

Art smiled. "Mona's not much for grieving."

"You'll tell Chuck and Wes that you'll let us go?"

"No, I can't. Pa wants them both dead."

Rosalie stared at him. Nothing made sense.

"You want to murder Chuck and our ranch hand, and then expect me to marry you?"

"Ranch hand? I heard you were smitten with him."

Rosalie did not want Wes in any further danger. "Wes is our ranch hand, that's all." Rosalie stared into the fire. She knew she was in a bad spot.

Art smiled at her. "Forget about Montana. He's going to be dead by morning. And you and me, we'll take over the south mesa."

Rosalie knew she had to be careful. She avoided his gaze.

"What about Chuck?"

"You're the only one we need." He stood close and bent down to touch her hair.

"Mona won't let you hurt her son," Rosalie said.

Art grinned, shook his head, and had to tell her. "Mona's a determined woman. Ruthless, even."

"What do you mean?"

Art enjoyed telling her the truth. "Some time back, she came to me and Pa for help. She needed someone dead."

"I don't believe you."

"My father wanted to get the ranch through Mona, so he arranged it."

Rosalie waited, staring at him as he continued.

"It seems a few months back, a letter came from an Indian woman down in Arizona Territory at the Claymore ranch. She wrote she had Eastman's son. Said the boy didn't know who his father was. She wasn't gonna tell 'im until she knew if Eastman would own up."

Rosalie gripped her coffee cup, listening in silence. She remembered Wes's story about his mother, but she wasn't sure of the connection.

"Mona tore up the letter," Art said. "It was eating on her for a long time. She couldn't stand thinking the squaw might come to find Eastman. So my father told the Welsh brothers to get rid of her. They liked the big money but weren't happy about killing a woman, so they got their cousin Rango to go with 'em."

Art paused for effect as Rosalie looked stricken.

"Bad as he is, Rango didn't want to do it until he found out who she was."

"All three of them—"

"Sure, it was just another Indian. But we never got our hands on the son."

Rosalie knew what he was going to say next.

Art was enjoying himself. "But he came here anyhow."

"Wes Montana."

Art frowned. "How did you know?"

"I didn't."

"We sent for Rango again, but he's hard to find."

"This Rango, I heard he's ruthless."

"The worst, and he hates Montana. Seems Montana almost got him hanged once."

"So instead of facing up to Wes, he took it out on a helpless woman?"

Art frowned at her response. "Seems most everyone's afraid of Wes Montana. Even Rango. He'd never come after Montana 'less he had an army with him."

"Did Ray know this?"

"He's dead. What's the difference?"

"And Chuck knows Wes is his half brother?"

Art nodded. "Didn't you hear Mona tell Pa when we were outside? But Montana has no proof with his mother dead. So he won't get nothing."

"Ray would have done right by him."

"He's a half-breed," Art said.

"The best half could be Indian."

"He's a killer, Rosalie. Why do you think the cattlemen hired him up in Wyoming? To hang rustlers."

"Like Rango."

Art leaned over, stroked her arm. She recoiled.

"Rosalie, when you marry me—"

"I will not do that."

"You have no choice."

"Yes, I do. As soon as the storm breaks, I'm leaving."

"You might get hurt."

"But you know they will come for me."

"That's the plan."

"Someone may be killed."

"Also part of the plan."

"Art, is it worth it?"

"We need more grass and all that water."

"But you'll hang for it."

He shook his head. "Who can blame us for killing anyone who comes here and attacks our ranch?"

"You're just like your father."

He grinned. She tried to find words to dissuade him, but could not. She was exhausted. Rosalie listened to the storm, gathered her blanket around her, and fell asleep on her chair.

Later that night at the Rodecker ranch house, Mona, still fully dressed, waited on the porch in the dark as Pete came up the steps. Lamplight filtered from the shuttered windows. The storm was loud. Rain poured off the porch roof.

Pete shook the rain from his hat and removed his slicker.

Mona hurried to greet him, kissing him passionately.

"Ray's dead." She stroked his arm. "The ranch is mine. As soon as I've grieved enough, we can have that grand wedding."

"I changed my mind."

"What?"

"We found out Eastman changed his will some time ago. All you get is money, a lot of it. But Rosalie and Chuck get the ranch. And the ranch is what I want. As soon as Rosalie marries Art."

"You're lying."

"Money buys good information."

He pushed her away. She fell back a step.

"Ray loves me. He wouldn't—"

"Probably figured you didn't like living there."

"But I was his wife."

"Were you?"

She made a move to slap him but didn't.

"Regardless, we don't need you," he said.

She was frightened by what she saw in his face.

"But you said if I was free—"

"You think I'd marry a dangerous woman like you? I could be next on your list."

Mona was so shattered, she whined. "But you said you loved me."

"We had our fun. But no one loves a rattlesnake."

"I let Ray die for you."

"Ah, so it comes out."

"You can't do this to me."

"Sorry, but my wife's in Denver. She left me ten years ago because she caught me with another woman."

"You said she died a long time ago."

"Just a story. When we have the whole mesa, I'll go to Denver and court her all over again."

It took her a moment to realize how well she'd been tricked. Fury welled up within her. "Rosalie won't marry Art. You won't get any land from her or Chuck."

He sneered. "You've been jealous of how pretty and young she is, you'll be like the wicked witch and lock her in the attic?"

Mona nodded. "Anything to stop you."

"You can go, but Rosalie stays."

"Chuck won't let you get your hands on her."

"Chuck won't be around."

Mona was insulted and hateful but her son? Pete wanted to kill her son? She slapped him hard on the face.

His head snapped back. He merely grinned.

Danger flashed in her eyes. "I suppose you have plans to silence me as well," she said.

"Why should I bother? You know if you make trouble, everyone will hear how you had that Indian murdered. If you don't keep your mouth shut, you'll hang."

"So will you."

"I didn't arrange it. You did."

"Wes Montana finds out, he'll kill everyone."

"I sent for Rango. He won't come alone."

"You'll all be dead before he ever gets here," she snapped. Furious, she left him and hurried into the house.

He chuckled and turned away.

The storm continued to bring dark, heavy rain.

Mona charged into the Rodecker house and stopped. Alone in the parlor, Rosalie, blankets around her, slept on a chair by the fire.

Mona tried to wipe off her murderous look; she dabbed at her eyes, put on a sweet face, and walked over to Rosalie. She put her hand on Rosalie's arm.

Rosalie sat up straight and looked up at her. Rosalie recoiled from her touch, remembering what Art had said, yet she needed Mona to help her escape.

"I'm so sorry about all this," Mona said.

Mona pulled up a chair near Rosalie.

"You should not marry Art. You deserve better."

"I never wanted—"

"And Pete, he was after me all this time, but now I find out his wife's still alive and in Denver. They are all liars."

Rosalie took a long moment to digest Mona's words. "I wish we'd never met either one of them," Rosalie said. "We lost Ray and now they want to kill Chuck and Wes."

"Yes, dear, I know. It's very painful for both of us. Now get some sleep. Maybe we can think of something tomorrow."

"I tried to get out a back window, but some nasty men stopped me." Very sleepy, Rosalie closed her eyes.

Mona turned grim, got up, and took the stairs up to her room.

Rosalie opened her eyes, watching Mona until she was out of sight.

She knew Mona had orchestrated the death of Wes's mother. She was a woman Rosalie had never liked, and now she knew why.

But they needed each other. Wes and Chuck would be riding into an ambush. Something had to be done.

Chapter Ten

Late that night in the heavy rain, in a grove of trees not far from the Rodecker ranch house, Wes, Chuck, and Travers dismounted. They wore only heavy coats, and they were getting soaked. Rain ran off their hat brims. They worried about lightning.

They were on a rise with a good view in all directions. They saw Clem and Thor Welsh, wearing slickers, on the steps. And saw movement of two men standing under the barn roof's overhang. Horses nervously moved around the corrals.

Wes gestured. "That's Rosalie's mare."

Chuck studied the scene. "I count maybe a half-dozen guns, over by the barn and corrals, waiting for us."

"I can get around behind the house," Travers said, "keep 'em inside."

"Good idea," Wes said. "If we could get down there without being seen . . ."

"Hold it," Chuck said.

They watched as Pete and Art came out of the house, but they could not hear what was said. They were too far away, and the rain was loud.

Unaware they were being watched from the rise, the Welsh brothers, rolling smokes, guarding the ranch house, stood at the foot of the steps and under the porch overhang, out of the rain. Art and Pete were standing farther back on the porch. Pete had his cigar.

Thor nodded to the darkness. "They ain't coming."

Art disagreed. "If they're alive, they'll be here. I'd say, about dawn. But they'll wait till the storm passes."

Pete nodded. "We may as well get some sleep."

Art looked at the Welsh brothers. "Keep a good watch," he said.

"What about Rango?" Thor asked.

"I sent word," Pete replied, "but it seems your cousin has some posse on his trail."

Thor grinned. "He does keep 'em busy."

"You'll have to handle Montana," Art said.

"He's only one man," Thor said with bravado.

Pete and Art went back inside. The Welsh brothers took seats on the porch. Thor pulled out a bottle of whiskey.

"Just as well," Thor said. "Rango's kin, but he's one bad son of a gun."

Clem nodded. "You think he really skinned somebody alive?"

"I believe it."

"He sure hates Wes Montana, but he's scared of him."

"Don't ever tell him that."

They both grinned. Shared their whiskey.

"Come to think of it," Clem said, sobering, "I'm plenty scared of Montana myself."

"Yeah, but he don't have eyes in the back of his head."

"He won't know what hit him."

Both grinned and chuckled. Looking at the rain, they seemed content.

At the Rodecker ranch in the heavy rain, while Travers made his way around the house to take cover, Chuck and Wes slipped into the barn from the right, both on foot. They got in through an open window, then dropped down into the stalls.

Chuck and Wes saw two heavily armed men by the front barn door, which was open. They were standing inside, just out of the rain.

Wes signaled Chuck to stay put and cover him. He slipped along the stalls, then ducked into one near the two men. Wes could see past them to where two other men stood in the shelter of a lean-to by the trough. The lean-to had only side walls and a roof. They were having a smoke. They looked like gunmen. Two other men sheltered over by a wagon next to the barn. The rain did not let up. It was dark and miserable.

Wes stepped out of the stall behind the two men at the door. He spoke low.

"Move back inside." He moved closer. "Drop your gun belts."

The two men did not care enough to fight. There wasn't enough money to take on Wes Montana. They moved back into the barn, unbuckling their gun belts as Chuck hurried to join Wes. Chuck took some rope from a hook on the wall.

"Tie 'em good," Wes said.

Chuck got busy as Wes peered out of the barn. "I'll take care of those at the lean-to. You cover me."

Wes, buckskin straps in his belt, slipped up behind the two seated on the trough under the lean-to. He grabbed them both from behind, by the neck, and slammed their heads together, knocking them out. He lowered them to the ground, out of the rain and out of sight of the others. He took their weapons and threw them in the trough. Then he rolled them on their sides and tied their hands and feet.

Wes slid back into the barn where Chuck was waiting.

"Two more at the wagons," Chuck said. "I know that one with the conchas on his hat. He's called Remms."

Wes shoved his six-gun at the temple of one of the two prisoners Chuck was watching.

The two men had no taste for any more trouble.

"Call 'em in here," Wes said. "Say you got whiskey."

The prisoner nodded his head rapidly.

Wes removed the barrel to let him stick his head out of the

door and call to the other men.

The prisoner called out. "Hey, fellas, come and have a drink." Poked by Wes's gun, "Got a whole bottle."

Chuck took the prisoners aside and sat them down in a stall. As the other two men hurried through the rain and into the dark barn, they were met with guns in their ribs.

Wes spoke quietly. "Drop your gun belts and you won't get hurt."

Chuck began pushing Remms around.

"Maybe you was in on killing Wes's mother," Chuck said.

"No," said Remms.

"Who was it?" Chuck demanded.

Remms didn't answer, just looked nasty. With his hands tied behind him, ankles bound, seated against a stall, Remms glared up at them.

Wes grabbed Remms by the nose and shoved the barrel of his six-gun into the man's mouth.

"Who was it?" Wes demanded.

Remms turned chicken. He tried to talk. Wes withdrew his pistol to the man's lips and let go of his nose.

Remms coughed out his words. "The Welsh brothers. And their cousin, Rango. They bragged about it."

Wes was hot with fury. "Rango? Is he here?"

"Ain't seen 'im."

"What about our two hands we found in the hills?" Chuck demanded.

"Welsh brothers did that."

While two gunmen were bound in the lean-to and four others were tied and gagged in the barn, Clem and Thor leaned their rifles against the porch rail and sat on benches near the front door.

Lamplight filtered out through the shuttered windows. Rain was still heavy in a black night.

"Black rain," Thor grunted.

Both men were half-asleep as they finished their smokes.

"I'm right hungry," Thor said.

"The boss might get mad. Better wait."

Daybreak brought the sun. Clouds hovered but were passing quickly with the wind. The mud was heavy all around.

Clem and Thor had both been dozing on the porch bench. The two men stretched and yawned. When they sat up straight, they were startled.

Wes and Chuck appeared facing the porch from about ten feet away. Both aimed six-guns at Clem and Thor.

Wes knew they had been in on his mother's murder. It would be easy to pull the trigger, ease his agony. The Welsh brothers rose from their seats.

Wes gestured. "Don't move a hair. Drop your gun belts."

"You're going to hang," Chuck said.

Clem and Thor could feel their rope burns under their bandannas. Both of them would rather die any other way, and this was the time to face it.

Clem bristled. "We didn't do anything."

"My folks are dead," Chuck said. "So I figure I'll hang you myself. Ever see a man at the end of a rope? Kicking and squealing? If you're lucky, your neck will break right off."

Wes figured Chuck had never seen a hanging, but he sure liked his spunk.

Both Thor and Clem knew how it really felt.

Thor grimaced. "We don't know nothing about your pa, but your ma's inside."

Chuck, startled, reacted with some relief. But he saw Wes was ready to kill them.

"You murdered Wes's mother," Chuck said.

"We was there, but Rango done it."

"We oughta just kill 'em right now," Chuck said.

But Wes could not murder in cold blood.

Clem and Thor seemed to sense this. They had tricked other men before and were already sharing the same thoughts.

Wes glared at the men. "I said drop them gun belts."

"Yeah," Chuck said, "or we'll start on your boots, then your knees and maybe where you're real ugly."

Thor, taking him serious, began to sweat.

Clem was determined not to die hanging. "We can end it right here, if you're of a mind. Fair and square."

"Go ahead," Thor said, "shoot us in cold blood, or take your chances."

Clem and Thor started for the steps. Wes and Chuck backed farther away from the porch. Sunlight gleamed on their weapons.

Thor and Clem, more terrified of hanging than a gunfight, even with Wes Montana, came off the steps and moved around to face Wes and Chuck.

"What'll it be?" Clem demanded.

Slowly Wes and Chuck holstered their weapons. Instantly, the gunmen drew and fired.

Wes drew fast, was hit high on the left shoulder by Clem's bullet. Wes's bullet killed Thor.

Chuck drew and killed Clem, whose shot had missed Chuck. The startled gunmen fell and rolled in the mud. Two of the men who had murdered Mary Antelope lay dead at last. Wes felt no relief.

Wes was bleeding at the left shoulder. He and Chuck looked around.

No one was coming from the cook shed or the bunkhouse.

They heard shots behind the house.

"Someone tried to get out," Chuck said. "Hope Travers is okay."

"If he is, they'll be coming out the front. Get ready."

"You've been shot," Chuck said.

Chuck yanked off his own bandanna and shoved it inside Wes's shirt against the wound. Wes nodded his thanks, kept his own hand on it.

Chuck backed away, looked at the house, heard noise.

There was a commotion inside the Rodecker house. Art and Pete had peered out the side window at the fight. Mona held back in her fury. There was no sign of Anna.

Rosalie bolted for the door.

Art spun around and grabbed Rosalie, keeping his arm around her neck as she fought him.

Mona hurried to help Rosalie.

Pete grabbed Mona by the arm, socked her on the jaw, and threw her against the wall. Mona slammed against the wall and slid to the floor, stunned.

Art dragged Rosalie toward the front door. Pete was right behind them.

As they went outside, Mona, still dazed but furious, stood and picked up a poker from the hearth. She staggered forward, full of hate for being scorned, for the shame of it, the embarrassment. And there was no way she'd let them kill Chuck. Mona gripped the poker and headed for the front door.

Coming out of a back room, Anna was startled, held back.

Mona didn't see Anna. She was in a hurry.

Outside the Rodecker house, the door opened to the porch in the bright sun. Art came out, his arm around Rosalie's neck, near choking her. She clawed at his arm, unable to reach his face.

The barrel of his six-gun was pressed against the side of her head. Rosalie struggled as her breath left her. She began to collapse in Art's grip.

Wes and Chuck stood in the mud, staring up at them.

Art sneered. "Now listen carefully. Both of you. Drop your guns."

Wes and Chuck slowly obeyed, careful to set their weapons on the porch steps, out of the mud.

"Now," Art said, "back off. Rosalie and me, we got a date with a preacher."

Wes and Chuck backed farther away from their weapons. Behind Art, Pete appeared with a six-gun in hand. Behind Pete, a vicious Mona appeared with a poker. Pete did not see her. Nor did Art. Pete gestured toward the corrals, saw no one.

"We need a wagon. Where are the men?"

"Kind of tied up," Chuck said.

Pete snickered and aimed at Chuck. "All right, we'll end it now. Say your prayers, kid."

Mona was dark with fury as she lifted the poker and slammed Pete on the head with a loud crack. Pete stumbled and dropped to his knees, stunned. He rolled on the porch, fired up, and hit Mona in the chest. She doubled up, collapsed, and fell into a heap.

Pete got to his feet, staggering, dazed but still with his six-gun in hand. He aimed at Mona again.

Travers appeared at the other end of the porch. He fired and hit Pete dead center. Pete crumpled to the porch, dead.

Art still held Rosalie around the neck. Of a sudden, Anna was on Art from behind, clawing at his face and eyes. Art fought to hold the six-gun and Rosalie.

Rosalie, freed slightly, bit Art's arm. He yelped. She broke free, shoved and kicked Art, then fell to her knees.

Anna shoved Art away from Rosalie, kicking him in the leg.

Wes, leaping onto the porch, pounced on Art. They fought furiously, pounding each other. They fell from the porch and rolled in the mud.

Chuck hurried to recover their weapons. He holstered his

and held Wes's in each hand.

Wes slammed his fist in Art's face. Art clawed at his eyes.

Anna pulled Rosalie to safety, back on the porch where Pete and Mona lay dead. Rosalie was crying at the sight of Mona.

Travers obliged, lifted Mona and carried her body back inside. Then he came back outside with a blanket and threw it over Pete.

Chuck, his own weapon holstered and Wes's in his hands, hovered around the two fighting men.

Wes, badly wounded, strength ebbing, punched Art. Art slammed a fist onto Wes's wounded shoulder, and Wes fell in agony. Art's other hand was on his six-gun as he rolled over and pointed at the wounded Wes.

Chuck pulled the trigger. His bullet hit Art dead center. Art rolled over on his back, arms flailing, then lay dead.

Wes sat up, trying to stop the flow of blood from his wound. He staggered to his feet as Chuck hurried to help him onto the steps, then onto the porch, where Anna and Rosalie led him to a bench. Chuck slid Wes's guns back into their holsters.

Rosalie sat at Wes's side as Anna went for water and towels.

Chuck stood beside her. Rosalie tried to open Wes's shirt, yanking at it.

Wes muttered. "You're killing me."

She fussed. "Don't be a baby."

Wes made a face, couldn't help his fondness for her.

Travers walked down the steps with Chuck.

Seven ranch hands were coming from the range. They reined up near the porch. They were cowhands, not looking for a fight.

Chuck stood tall, facing the riders.

"Haul off your dead, and there won't be no trouble. You get that done, send those killers in the barn and lean-to on their way, without their guns. But give 'em their horses."

The men appeared relieved.

Chuck continued. "When the dust settles, the whole mesa will be the Eastman ranch. There'll be jobs for all of you what haven't done no killing."

The hands nodded their thanks. Travers volunteered to help them.

As the morning advanced, Wes remained on the Rodecker porch bench as Anna and Rosalie worked to stop the bleeding in his shoulder.

Sitting upright, he swayed. Rosalie's arm went around his back to hold him steady.

"Ease up," Wes said.

"Such a baby," Rosalie responded.

Wes would never let on that he was enjoying every minute of her attention. He knew that he was still a half-breed and would never have her true affection. He could never have a life with such a woman, ever.

At the same time, his half brother was a joy.

Chuck helped Rosalie. "He's still leaking," Chuck said. "Maybe we need to burn some gunpowder on it."

"No," Rosalie said.

"It will stop," Anna said, rising. "I'll bring more bandages." She smiled. "Tearing up Rodecker sheets." Anna went back into the house.

Chuck sat back and grinned at Wes.

"Two pretty women fussing over you. How lucky can you get?"

Wes grimaced, but inside, he was smiling.

Chuck looked eastward, then got to his feet. "Look," he said.

They followed his gaze to an approaching chuck wagon with a half-dozen riders and a dog trailing.

On the wagon seat was Jones, driving, with Ray Eastman next to him.

Chuck gasped. "It's Pa!"

The chuck wagon pulled up near the porch. Chuck hurried down the steps, over to the wagon. He reached up and grabbed Eastman's hand.

"It's over, Pa. The Rodeckers are dead."

Eastman saw Rosalie with Wes on the porch.

Anna was inside the house and unseen.

Eastman was grim. "Where's your mother?"

"She's dead," said Chuck. "Pete shot her."

Jones got down and came around the wagon. He and Chuck helped the weary Eastman down from the wagon and over to the porch, guiding him up the steps to the bench where he sat next to Wes and Rosalie.

The dog stayed at the bottom of the steps to watch.

Jones paused on the porch to look down at Wes.

"You're a mess," Jones said with a grin.

"Getting worse," Wes said, glaring at Rosalie as she adjusted the bloody bandage. "I'd be better off with a horse doctor."

"Maybe," Jones agreed with a grin.

"Only doctor around's the barber," Chuck said.

Wes tried to relax as Rosalie stopped working on him.

"You boys did all right," Eastman said.

Jones went back down the steps, climbed on the chuck wagon, and turned it toward the barn, with the riders following.

Chuck gathered himself together, fighting for his words.

"The Welsh brothers are dead. It was them and Rango killed Wes's mother, but nobody knows where Rango is."

"I'll find him," Wes said.

"No," Eastman told him, "it could take years."

"Wes, we need you here," Chuck said.

"I got two sons now," Eastman said. "Let's keep it that way."

"Rodecker sent for Rango," Chuck said. "Let him come to us."

Wes was too weak from bleeding to argue further.

Rosalie looked warily at Eastman, unsure how to avoid hurting him. She spoke softly.

"It was Mona who received the letter. It must have worried her, so she went to Pete Rodecker. He sent the Welsh brothers, and they brought in Rango."

Eastman looked drained. Rosalie added more.

"But just now, at the last minute, Mona tried to help. She came after Pete with a poker. Whacked him on the head. He's the one who shot her. And Mr. Travers shot him."

"Wes and me, we got the Welsh brothers," Chuck said, "but Wes, he didn't duck. But you should have seen him fighting hand to hand with Art and bleeding all the time."

"Chuck got Art," Wes said.

Chuck looked suddenly tired. "Pa, we were really worried about you."

Eastman showed the amulet. "Mary saved my life. With this."

Wes, Chuck, and Eastman gazed at each other with a connection that was growing by the minute.

Anna came outside with more bandages. When he got a good look at the beautiful Anna, Eastman was startled and dumbfounded.

Anna was a walking tornado with beauty and fire in her eyes.

Ray had never before seen anyone like her.

Rosalie held Wes with one arm as Anna worked on the wound.

Eastman moved closer to Wes. He reached over and squeezed Wes's good arm.

Wes looked at Rosalie's smile and realized that she already knew he was Eastman's son, a half-breed. Wes saw no disdain in her gaze, her shining eyes.

Eastman kept staring at Anna as she helped Wes.

"Ray," Rosalie said, "during the fight, Art had me by the neck, but Anna grabbed him, made him let me go." She hesitated. "And now she needs a job."

Eastman swallowed hard. "Why, uh . . ."

"I told her we'd hire her," Rosalie said.

"Yeah, sure," Eastman said, stymied.

"She needs to earn enough to bring her children here. They're in some children's home near Salt Lake."

Eastman felt a tug at his heart. He knew what it was like in an orphanage—the tyrants in charge, the scant meals, the sleepless nights that were too cold, the work forced on them, being treated like slaves. A place he had escaped at fourteen, never to look back. And now this beautiful Mexican woman had to rescue her own children from such a prison.

"I think we should advance her enough," Rosalie said.

"Yeah, sure," Eastman said.

"I'll go with her. We'll take the stage."

"Okay, sure," Eastman said, unable to take his eyes from Anna. He had been far too long without the love of a woman, which had been denied to him by his own wife.

Wes winced as the women worked on his wounds.

"What about Rodecker's stock?" Wes asked.

Before Eastman could figure it out, Rosalie spoke up.

"He has a wife in Denver."

"That's it then," Eastman said. "We'll get his cattle and horses sold to the army and send the money to her."

"She deserves it," Rosalie said. "And Anna deserves her own children."

At Salt Creek, south of Salt Lake, the Salt Creek Children's Home raised vegetables for sale. The children housed there worked hard in the fields, digging, planting, and harvesting.

Rosalie saw this as she and Anna pulled up in a rented wagon a week after the battle at the Rodecker ranch.

"My boys," Anna said, pointing to the fields.

At that moment, a heavy-set house mistress with a fat nose, Mrs. Jonas, chased a young blond girl out of the building.

"You get back in here and scrub that floor, and do it right this time."

The girl was about sixteen and had long golden hair, a trim figure, and large blue eyes. She was wearing a faded dress. She had bruises on her face and wrists.

Mrs. Jonas chased the tearful girl back inside, then turned as Anna and Rosalie stepped down and came up to the steps.

"This is Anna Gomez," Rosalie said. "She's here for her children. I'm Rosalie Riley."

"Yes," Mrs. Jonas said. "I got your letter. I have their accounts all totaled."

"Who was that blond girl?" Rosalie asked.

"That's Molly Jones. Nothing but trouble."

"She could come with us."

Mrs. Jonas looked her over. "She's been here for years. No one wants her because her accounts are more than they can afford."

"Tell me what they are."

"You may not want her. She's wicked."

"Can I talk to her?"

Mrs. Jonas hesitated. Molly had become a hard-working servant and there was no one to replace her.

"Her family dumped her here when she was small," Mrs. Jonas said. "They had seven boys and no use for a girl. Besides she was sickly. They signed the papers. We never heard from them again, and there is a very large account that needs to be paid."

"If it's reasonable, I can write a bank draft," Rosalie said, "but I'd like to speak with her."

Mrs. Jonas made a disgruntled face and went back inside.

Anna stared at her boys in the field; unable to contain herself, she ran toward them. There were twins of six and of eight, and the ten-year-old. Healthy but miserable, until they saw their mother and ran toward her.

Rosalie was tearful as she saw Anna reach them in the middle of the crops and drop to her knees to hug the five little boys.

Then Mrs. Jonas forced Molly outside.

"Molly, this woman wants to buy your accounts."

Rosalie smiled at the girl. "Do you want to come with us?"

Molly hesitated as tears filled her eyes.

"I promise," Rosalie said, "you will be happy with us."

Mrs. Jonas was torn between payment and losing a servant.

Rosalie held out her arms.

Molly sobbed and hurried into Rosalie's embrace.

Mrs. Jonas snickered at Rosalie. "I hope you have a lot of money. She'll be hard to replace." Cold. "Come to my office." Mrs. Jonas stalked back inside.

Molly stepped back from Rosalie, wiping at her eyes.

"She treats you like a servant," Rosalie said. "Does she beat you?"

Molly looked frightened. "Don't say that to her."

"Well, let's go inside and get you free."

A short time later, Molly, Rosalie, and Anna with her five boys left the children's home and walked to the wagon. The boys scrambled in back.

Molly looked hesitant.

"Don't worry," Rosalie said, "you're going to a very fine ranch run by very nice people. You will help me and Anna in the house, and that's all."

Molly hugged Anna and teased the boys a little. They obviously loved Molly, as one grabbed her hand.

"I'll send off a letter, but we're going shopping before we do anything else," Rosalie said. "All of you need some new clothes and a rest before we go back on the stage."

Molly's eyes sparkled. She was beaming.

Anna was worried. "But it's Mr. Eastman's money."

Rosalie laughed. "He signed the drafts and said I could spend all I needed."

A few days later at the Eastman ranch on the mesa, Ray Eastman, Chuck, and Wes, his arm in a sling, shared a breakfast in the ranch house.

"Chuck," Eastman said, "you're a lousy cook."

"Sure be glad when Rosalie's back," Chuck agreed. "But her letter said as how she had to cash another draft and never even said what for."

"I'm not worried," Eastman said.

Chuck grinned. "Or even how many children Anna has."

"Just so she's a good cook," Eastman said.

"We got to get to Claymore's before the snow comes," Wes said.

"I'm going with you," Chuck said. "Jones can handle the place, now Rodeckers are gone."

Eastman nodded. "Especially since Bates's newspaper says Rango was killed down in Tucson."

"I wanted to hang him," Wes said.

"Just so he's dead," Eastman said.

Wes could not handle Rango's having escaped Wes's wrath. It was eating at him, deep and painful.

Eastman felt the same, but he settled back, enjoying his two sons. He listened as Wes and Chuck talked about the mares and what stallion they might buy.

In spite of Mona's treachery, he was a happy man.

Two weeks later, Ray Eastman was back in the saddle as he and his sons rode up to the Claymore ranch in Arizona Territory. It was a cold but sunny day.

Wes, Eastman, and Chuck stepped down as the Claymores came out to greet them.

"This is my pa, and my brother, Chuck," Wes said.

"You're Ray Eastman," Claymore said, shaking his hand.

"We need to talk," Eastman said to Claymore, who nodded.

At that moment, Haley rode from the corrals at a lope. He was on his old horse. He reined up, swung down, and hurried to shake Wes's hand.

"This is Jim Haley," Wes said to Eastman and Chuck.

"Yeah, we heard about you," Eastman said to the boy.

"We adopted him," Claymore said. "He's our son now."

Haley was beaming.

"But," Claymore said with a grin, "that's still the oldest horse I ever saw." He chuckled. "Best dang cow pony on the place."

That night for supper at the Claymore ranch house, Jim Haley was at the table with the Claymores, Wes, Chuck, and Ray Eastman.

"Jim's doing well in school," Claymore said.

Wes felt a bit envious when he saw the old man's pride in the teenager. Wes had never felt that affection, or maybe he had shrugged it away as an angry youth trying to escape the name-calling and finding his own way in life, but he was happy for Haley.

When Mrs. Claymore and Jim Haley had retired for the night, Ross Claymore gave his attention to Ray Eastman's grief. As Wes listened, Claymore told him how well-loved Mary had been at church, at school, and in the good deeds she had done for others. He also told him she had turned down many marriage proposals.

"She told me," Claymore said to Eastman, "that she had already had her one true love, and he had died. She thought you were dead."

★ ★ ★ ★ ★

That night at Mary's graveside in the dark, Wes and Eastman stood alone. It was a cold but starry night. Wes had already been through his grief at the marker, but it still hurt, and he could see his father was suffering.

"I'd have given my life for her," Eastman said.

"She never wanted anyone else," Wes replied.

Wes could see his father was breaking down.

Eastman went down on his knees. His body was shaking.

Wes put his hand on Eastman's shoulder, then turned and went back inside, leaving his father to his grief.

Weeks later, back on the mesa, Eastman spent most of his time in the saddle. Day and night, he enjoyed being with Chuck and Wes. They increased their herd, sold off the Rodecker scrubs, and put the money in the bank for transfer to the widow in Denver.

They had a dozen mares ready for breeding but no stallion as yet.

They built fence, cleaned the ponds, leveed the river in bad spots. Winter was coming. Rosalie's letters told of time spent shopping in Salt Lake, but she promised to be home soon.

Weeks later, on a dreary winter's day under a dark sky, Jones met the stage in town. After gathering his passengers, he drove the wagon up to the mesa and over to the ranch house. Anna and Rosalie, both in new clothes and wearing hooded cloaks, sat beside him. It was drizzling and cold.

In back with all their belongings, five little Mexican boys were roughhousing. They had new clothes and hats. They wore heavy coats that didn't stop them from pushing each other around as they laughed. Trying to handle the boys was Molly, who wore a pretty dress under a big coat. Her golden hair was blowing about her face.

Rosalie slid down from the wagon, then helped Anna step down.

Shorty came hobbling over from the bunkhouse.

"Mr. Ray is out with his sons," Shorty said.

"Shorty," Rosalie said, "this is Molly. She was all alone, so we brought her along."

"Welcome, Miss Molly," Shorty said.

"And Anna's boys," Rosalie added.

Shorty grinned at the boys who were scrambling down from the back of the wagon with Molly.

Jones and Shorty exchanged glances, both tickled that Eastman and his sons were going to get one heck of a surprise.

It was starting to rain, hard. The boys, with Molly on their heels, ran for the porch.

Rosalie and Anna grabbed carpet bags and ran to follow.

Jones and Shorty unloaded the rest of their belongings.

Arriving back at the ranch in the late afternoon of the same day, weary from their latest work on the mesa, Eastman, Chuck, and Wes unsaddled in the barn. It was still raining.

"Been a long day," Eastman said, then grinned. "And a lot longer when you start getting old."

"You ain't old, Pa," Chuck said. "You can still outride us."

"You bet your boots I can."

Wes and Chuck looked at each other in amusement.

"Sure am hungry," Chuck said. "But it ain't my turn to cook."

Before they could answer, Jones came in to greet them.

"Rosalie and Miss Anna are in the house," Jones said.

"I smell bread baking," Chuck said. "About time."

Jones grinned. He had no intention of warning them about the five rambunctious boys and the pretty teenage Molly.

Eastman and his sons left their slickers on the porch and

shook rain from their hats as they walked into the house.

They smelled hot bread and sniffed the air with delight.

There was a fire in the hearth but no one around.

Eastman flopped on the couch, warming himself.

Wes and Chuck sat down on chairs, stretched, and yawned.

Rosalie came out of the kitchen with Anna.

Rosalie was tickled to see them both.

"Glad you're back," Rosalie said, giving Eastman, then Chuck, a hug.

Rosalie looked at Wes, who quickly stoked the fire.

Eastman gaped at Anna, so rosy and pretty.

"Smells good in here," Eastman said with a weak smile.

Just then, five little boys ran out of a back room with stick guns, stumbled to a halt, stared up at Chuck, and went racing out of the room.

Eastman sat up, startled.

"Yes," Rosalie said, "five boys. The oldest is ten. There are two sets of twins, six and eight."

Chuck was grinning. "Well, Pa, we got our hands full."

Anna met Eastman's gaze, blushed, and went back into the kitchen.

Chuck was getting a kick out of Eastman's infatuation.

Until he looked up the stairs as Molly came slowly down, golden hair around her shoulders, a vision of loveliness in gingham he could scarce accept.

Rosalie came to his side.

"Molly is sixteen. She was at the orphanage, but they were using her like a servant and didn't want to let her go. That's why it took so long. And why we needed more money."

Chuck was turning red, even as he nodded to Molly.

Eastman was overwhelmed, but he was still a happy man. *My God,* he thought as he leaned closer to the warm fire, *what a blessing. Everyone here. And Anna. Almost like when I met Mary.*

He sobered. *Maybe blessings aren't meant to last. We get our fill and take it all for granted, instead of taking hold and never letting go of it.*

Eastman was deep in thought as others chattered.

Chapter Eleven

A week later at the Eastman ranch, it was a quiet evening. Night was falling. Stars began to glitter. It had not rained for several days.

Eastman sat alone on the porch bench. He had no light in the porch lantern. Just a peaceful twilight turning into night.

Over by the smithy, Shorty, Jones, and Wes were playing soft, sweet music. Eastman listened a long while, enjoying it. Finally, the music stopped.

Eastman grinned as he heard kids laughing in the house.

Jones came over from the smithy and up the steps.

They listened to the noise inside.

Jones grinned. "I hear Anna's been teaching Chuck and Molly how to dance. Those kids really like each other."

"They're a match, all right. Someday."

"What about you and Anna?"

"A little too soon."

"You don't marry her, I will."

"What?"

"I sure wouldn't let any grass grow under my feet."

"All right, I get the message."

Jones was grinning. "Molly and Chuck. You and Anna. And all those kids."

Eastman nodded. "And what about Rosalie and Wes?"

Jones grinned. "He's scared silly of her."

"Got to fix that."

Jones turned and headed back over to the smithy.

Inside the house, Rosalie was clearing the table with Anna's help.

"That Mr. Ray," said Anna, "I would like him to like me."

"Are you kidding?" Rosalie asked. "He can't even talk when you're around. He's wild about you."

"I feel good with him."

"You said you have family in Mexico City?"

"My grandfather and some cousins."

"Maybe they would come to your wedding."

"When I marry a gringo?" Anna laughed.

"What's wrong with that?"

Anna sobered. "I came from a very important family. Everyone respected us. But I fell for a handsome vaquero who could barely read and write, and they refused to let me marry him. It was beneath us, they said. So we ran away together and married in this territory. My family disowned me. They are very proud."

"So you loved your husband," Rosalie said.

"More than life."

Rosalie touched her shoulder.

Anna wiped away a tear. "I will always love him. But everything's different now."

Anna began to smile again.

"The way I feel about Mr. Eastman, it is so wonderful, and he likes the boys, and he gets their names all mixed up, but they love him."

"He'll spoil them."

"It is time, is it not?"

"And," Rosalie added, "Chuck has really fallen for Molly. They are young, but someday . . ."

Anna smiled. “Someday.”

But Rosalie was thinking of Wes.

As Jones left for the smithy, Chuck had stepped outside to join his father on the porch. They sat alone and watched as Wes came from the corrals and then walked up the porch steps to join them.

At that moment, the five boys came running onto the porch. The oldest jumped on Eastman, bouncing around. The others tried to pull him off to take their turn.

Eastman was having fun until Molly came out and herded them back inside. Molly smiled at Chuck over her shoulder as she closed the door behind her.

Chuck was a mess and so in love.

Eastman mused. “It’s time we had a hoedown. Invite everyone in a hundred miles.”

Chuck grinned. “I’m for that. Take Anna, and I’ll take Molly.”

Wes was so happy it hurt. He had a father and a brother, and property. And possibly he would see Anna and Molly added to the family. Not to mention five little boys.

There was only one more thing he wanted, but he didn’t believe he would ever have Rosalie.

“Hey, Wes,” Chuck said, “you going to pop the question to Rosalie?”

“What’s this?” Eastman asked. “Behind my back?”

Wes flushed. “I wouldn’t embarrass you that way.”

Eastman frowned. “Because your mother was Arapaho? Be proud of her, Wes. Her people were from the land.”

“But Rosalie . . .”

Chuck grinned. “First time she saw you, she said she was going to marry you.”

Wes was too amazed to answer. Still, Rosalie hadn’t known the truth at the time.

"Course now you're Wesley Montana Eastman," Chuck added. "That would be Rosalie Ann Riley Montana Eastman. A mouthful."

The door opened. Rosalie, unaware of the conversation, came out, a shawl over her shoulders. She looked gorgeous in the moonlight.

Wes got to his feet. Chuck punched Wes on his good arm and then helped their father inside, closing the door behind them.

Alone with Rosalie in the moonlight, Wes felt nervous. Rosalie smiled, standing at his side.

Wes panicked. He started to retreat.

"Stop right there," she said.

Wes hesitated, awkward, hat in hand.

"You've been avoiding me. We're partners in this ranch, remember? Partners have to talk."

Wes shrugged, moving to go around her.

She took his arm and drew him back. He avoided looking down at her. Her touch was vibrating down to his boots.

"For a big bad gunfighter, you're scared to death of me."

Wes, still afraid of her, had no reply.

"Wes, everyone's afraid of you." She laughed. "But I'm not."

It took a while, but Wes found a few words.

"A beautiful woman, you could have anyone—"

"You think I'm beautiful?"

"You know you are."

"I only want to know that you think I am."

They stood on the porch, both searching for words.

There was a sudden chilling voice from the corrals.

"Montana, I'm waiting for you!"

Wes turned her from his arms.

He could not see anyone in the moonlight, but he knew the voice.

"Rango," he muttered.

"Thought I was dead?" Rango shouted. "You know a better way to get a posse off your tail?"

Wes gently shoved Rosalie.

"Get inside."

"You tried to hang me," Rango yelled.

"You need help," she said.

"Just hand me my gun belt."

"You killed my cousins," Rango shouted.

She hurried inside, but it was Eastman who brought out Wes's gun belt with twin holsters. Eastman was wearing his own gun belt.

Wes hurriedly strapped on his Colts, then tied down the holsters.

"You afraid of me?" Rango shouted.

"Chuck's gone out the back door," Eastman whispered.

"Pa, I have to do this alone. She was my mother."

"She was my wife."

Wes realized he had forgotten for a second his father's agony over Mary's death.

"You know blamed well Rango's got others with him," Eastman said. "He's over by the barn and has you set up."

"I know. But I don't want you hurt."

"Goes both ways."

Wes shrugged and started down the steps. Eastman was right beside him.

Horses in the barn were restless, snorting.

Rango appeared at the barn door.

At the window above where a rope was hanging, a rifle appeared.

Rango's pale eyes were like glass in the moonlight.

"Montana, this was a long time coming," Rango said. He came forward in the moonlight, hands near his twin holsters.

"I'm taking you in," Wes said.

Wes waved Eastman to the side and stood alone.

"You're going to hang," Wes added.

"You tried that once before."

Rango's eyes were ghostly, his smile vicious.

The rifle in the barn window suddenly flipped in the air and went sailing to the ground. It hit hard.

Chuck appeared in the window. He called, "He's down."

At that moment, Jones and Shorty appeared from the bunkhouse with rifles. Wes waved them back.

Rango knew he was in trouble, but with a display of bravado he came slowly toward Wes. At twenty feet away, he stopped. "You got too many on your side," Rango said. "You afraid of a fair fight?"

"With the man who murdered my mother?"

"You mean that Indian? She was real tasty."

Eastman, outraged, started forward, but Wes waved him back. "No, Pa, I'll handle this."

At the house, Rosalie, Anna, and Molly slipped onto the dark porch. Rosalie had a rifle. Anna held her back.

Moonlight gleamed on a rifle at the far end of the corrals. When Rosalie saw it, she lifted her rifle and fired.

The man was hit. He yelled, rose into view, and fired back, his shot hitting the post beside her.

Rosalie fired again. The man died on his feet, falling out of sight.

Wes and Eastman were startled to discover another rifle backing Rango's play, but they didn't turn their backs on Rango himself.

Rango let his nervous reaction show, then acted tough. He had one more rifle backing him.

When Eastman saw another rifle come around the barn, he drew and fired, hitting the man, who gasped and fell.

Wes was briefly distracted.

At the same moment, the desperate Rango drew and fired.

Jumping aside, Wes, too, drew and fired.

Rango's bullet shot by Wes's ear.

Wes's bullet hit Rango dead center.

Rango fired into the dirt. He had a strange look on his dying face. Slowly, he slid into a heap.

Wes was badly shaken, six-gun still in hand.

Eastman came to stand at Wes's side. He put his hand on Wes's shoulder.

"So it's over," Eastman said.

Chuck grabbed the dangling rope in front of the window. He was about to slide down when the man he had knocked out came to and leaped forward, knife in hand, and grabbed him.

Chuck clung to the rope and the man held onto him. They dangled and spun as they fought.

Wes and Eastman, weapons in hand, watched helplessly.

Chuck and the man struggled with the knife while Chuck tried to hang on to the rope.

Chuck's feet hit the barn wall, then kicked them out into space. When they hit the barn again, the knife went into the man's gut.

The dead man fell. Chuck slid down the rope, a cut on his arm. Molly cried out as Chuck fell to his knees. She ran down the steps and over to the barn, reaching him before Wes and Eastman did.

Chuck got to his feet. "I'm okay."

When Chuck saw Molly's tears, he suddenly went limp, grabbing his bleeding left arm.

"You're hurt," Molly whined.

Molly led Chuck past Wes and Eastman. Chuck looked back over his shoulder, grinning at them, then leaned on Molly with a moan. He allowed Molly to lead him up the steps, onto the porch past Rosalie, and into the house.

Seeing them together softened the pain for Wes and his father. They stared down at the dead Rango.

Jones and Shorty went to check the dead man alongside the barn. Then the one Chuck had downed.

Wes went to make sure the man at the corral was dead. He was impressed at how Rosalie had shot the man twice.

When he returned, Anna had reached Eastman and grabbed his arm. Eastman looked down at her tears.

"What are you crying about?"

"You old fool," Anna said.

"Hey, that's no way to talk to your employer."

"And why are you not my husband?" Anna demanded. "I have five boys who need a father. And I don't have a little girl."

Eastman, in shock, stared at her, his heart pounding. Then he turned and looked at the dead Rango.

The past was as dead as a man could let it be.

Eastman looked down at Anna. "You're right," he said.

"So what are you going to do about it?" she demanded.

Eastman grinned as he let her walk him back to the house and up the porch steps. Before they went through the door, Anna turned him about and moved into his arms as Rosalie watched.

Anna pulled Eastman's head down and kissed him. Stunned, he looked over at the smiling Rosalie, even as Anna led him into the house. Anna winked at Rosalie when Eastman wasn't looking.

They went inside and the door closed behind them.

Rosalie, alone on the porch, set her rifle aside.

She could see Wes at the corral, and she knew he was hurting.

Rosalie was so in love, she had to make things right.

She walked down the steps toward Wes, who was looking at the dead Rango. He looked tired, worn. His gun belt had never been heavier.

So much of the past was still heavy on his shoulders.

Letting go would be hard for a man used to violence.

Aware of Rosalie walking toward him in the moonlight, he tried to steel himself for unwanted sympathy.

He walked over to her to protect her from sight of the dead, something her gentle eyes had no right to see. He felt suddenly protective of her, and yet she had fired one of the fatal shots.

"It's over," he said.

"Your father is going to marry Anna."

Wes was surprised. It pleased him.

"At least something good will come of it," he said.

"And what about us?"

She moved closer. He was frantic.

"Rosalie, there's four dead men out here."

"I know," she said. "I got one of them."

Her matter-of-fact reply stunned him. Was there no end of surprises from this young woman? This girl who had a hold of his heart?

He turned to see Jones and Shorty checking the dead.

Jones waved to Wes that they would handle it.

Wes looked down at her shining eyes.

He wanted her so badly he could barely breathe, but she deserved better, he told himself.

"You called me Rosalie," she said, smiling up at him.

He shrugged and moved to go around her.

She blocked his path.

"You never said my name before," she told him.

She took his arm, turning him toward the house.

He let her hand fall away, moved on his own.

"Are you afraid of me?"

"I'm not for you," Wes said.

"What do you mean?"

"My mother was Arapaho."

"Is that all?" Rosalie laughed. "I thought you were avoiding me because I'm Irish."

Wes, startled, stared at her.

"Wes, your father's going to marry Anna. What's the difference?"

"But—"

"We own the whole mesa. Who's going to give us any trouble?"

"If anyone calls me a breed . . ."

She laughed softly. "Not to your face. Everyone's terrified of you. Except me."

She turned him to face her. He met her gaze and melted.

"You don't understand," he said. "I had to fight all my life because I was half Indian. I was still a kid when I took up the gun to make them leave me alone. After a time, my name was enough to make them back off. Even then, I knew what they were thinking, and it never goes away."

"Are you ashamed of being your mother's son?"

Wes was shamed by her question.

"No," he said.

"It made you stronger. Better. You have your father's grizzly ways and her gentle ones."

"I don't want you hurt by this."

"But, Wes," she said softly, "you make my heart sing."

Wes was overwhelmed, beaten down.

He felt the same way but didn't have the words. He couldn't believe this gorgeous young woman would even want to hold his hand.

As a boy, he had hated so much that love was a strange and painful experience. Fighting the world had made him hard, brutal, unfeeling.

Yet whenever he was around Rosalie, he was mush.

Like now.

He waited so long, she berated him.

"If you don't haul off and kiss me, we'll never get married. And then we won't have seven children. Or take that trip to San Francisco. Or grow old and watch our grandchildren playing in the garden, or swimming in the creek. And learning to ride with Ray yelling at them, and . . ."

Wes could only stare at her.

She pulled him close. "Kiss me or I'll never stop talking."

She stood on her tiptoes and drew his head down. Their lips met.

Thunder rolled through him as his knees gave way.

Wes was lost, barely able to stand. He put his arms around her and kissed her again. They embraced, breathless.

As she pressed her face to his chest, he held her tight, hand on her soft hair. His own heart was singing.

Rosalie's love, the way she hugged him, was well on its way to closing his violent, miserable past. He felt blessed.

He had a half brother who was a real kick. And Eastman, a man anyone would be proud to call father.

And now this young woman he had loved from first sight.

Never had he thought it would come to this.

Wes whispered thanks as he turned his gaze to the starry sky.

ABOUT THE AUTHOR

Lee Martin was born in Northern California and grew up on cattle ranches, raised in a family that participated in rodeos. Lee started writing in the third grade. Through the years, while working in the travel business and later becoming a lawyer, Lee has been a prolific writer of traditional Westerns. Lee has sold dozens of short stories as well as seventeen novels. Lee now writes full-time.

Lee's screenplay *Shadow on the Mesa* (based on this novel) was made into a Hallmark movie starring Kevin Sorbo that premiered in 2013 and became the second-highest-rated and second-most-watched original movie in the channel's network history. The movie won the Wrangler Award for best Western-themed television film and was released on DVD in 2013 to rave reviews.